CONTENTS

This book is dedicated to the memory of Sir Terry Pratchett who let me adapt one of his books into a play back in my younger days and supported me throughout. Although the phone-call to my college professor may have been a bit much.

His work still inspires me to think, laugh and imagine to this day.

STAR'S PROMISE

1. AWAKENING

Rafen awoke to the sound of silence. Cold sweat drenched his skin, and the bedding clung to him unpleasantly. As the dream faded, he slowly noticed the dull ache in his bones. He tried to sit up, but a wave of dizziness swept through him and the buzzing in his head grew all consuming. Falling back onto the bed, Rafen's head hit the soft pillow and sleep took him again.

Images flickered through his mind. Inky black liquid washed over his face and flooded his lungs. The water drowned jeers from his pilgrimage brothers out, rushing into his ears. Within the enveloping dark, he saw stars. Whether it was a vision or the last breath of air leaving his chest, he couldn't tell.

As Rafen struggled against the enveloping blackness, a sense of weightlessness overtook him. The mocking voices of his brothers seemed to stretch and distort, fading into the liquid abyss. His limbs flailed in a futile attempt to find something solid, but the only resistance came from the viscous fluid that filled his world.

Panic clawed at his mind as the stars in the darkness grew brighter, a cacophony of cold, distant lights. The beauty of the cosmos unfolded before him as suffocating terror gripped his heart.

With each breath, he encountered the bitter taste of the dark liquid, his attempts to breathe becoming more desperate. It seeped into every pore, every crevice, claiming him with an icy embrace. The sensation of drowning was absolute, yet, as his consciousness waned, a peculiar calmness settled over him.

But the tranquillity was short-lived. A new terror emerged from the void—the stars began to warp and twist, coalescing into a monstrous face that stared back at him with eyes as deep and unforgiving as black holes. Whispers of annihilation, of civilisations swallowed whole and worlds reduced to dust.

Rafen's heart raced. It was a glimpse into an abyss much darker. The entity's gaze promised not just the end of his life, but the obliteration of all he knew. The stars, once beacons of hope in the dark, now foretold a coming storm, a cataclysm that would sweep through the cosmos with merciless fury.

As the vision intensified, Rafen felt an overwhelming urge to scream, to break free from the insipid chill that filled his being. But no sound came; there was only the dark water and the cold, creeping dread of what was to come. The darkness closed in, and the stars blinked out one by one.

He woke again with a pounding head and his body shook as shivers wracked his weak frame. Rafen licked his lips, they were dry, but he didn't have the saliva to wet them. A soft pull drew his attention to his arm, and he reached over to test the soft cuff gripping his bicep. A small creature was strapped to his skin, its body segmented, with no obvious limbs or head. He carefully attempted to lift it away, but he found the thing was firmly attached. A sharp pain told Rafen that the strange insect was attached to him not just by the strap, but by teeth as well.

Try as he might, Rafen couldn't find the strength to remove the creature, so he turned his attention to the surrounding room. With great effort, he turned his head and a feeling of confusion flooded him. This wasn't his cell! The room was sparse, but comfortable, and for the first time, he noticed the softness of the mattress and the smoothness of the sheets against his skin. It felt unusual after years of sleeping on a hard bunk with raw, scratchy blankets.

Rafen's mind whirled with fragmented memories and disjointed thoughts. The strange voice in his head, the huge collision he felt back on the Divinium ship, the shouts, screams and choking sounds in the corridors around his cell and the silence that took hold as his former crew took their own lives one by one.

Then he remembered his conversation with the two strange women, so suspicious of him but ultimately so kind. Then nothing. He scrambled to gather his thoughts as he put together the last things before he must have blacked out. The strange voice in his head, no, it wasn't a voice as such. It felt more like someone directly implanting thoughts and words into his mind. It had a name, didn't it? That was it, it called itself Buddy. Buddy had told him they were here and could rescue him.

He had leapt at that chance without question. For so long, his world had been in that circular room, stale with his own stench and the muffled voices from outside his cell. They had long ago given up speaking to him directly when they realised he had no more prophecies to give them.

As he lay there, trying to piece together his recent past, the door to his room hissed softly open. A figure stepped inside, silhouetted against the dim light from the corridor. It was one of the women who had spoken to him before, her posture confident yet cautious. "Rafen," she said, her voice gentle but carrying an undercurrent of authority. "My name is Shanice. You're safe now, on board our ship."

Shanice approached slowly, giving Rafen time to adjust to her presence. He noticed a small device in her hand, which she pointed towards him. "This will help with the pain and the fever," she explained, pressing a button on the device. A soft, cool mist enveloped Rafen, and almost immediately, the pounding in his head eased, and the shivering subsided. "And don't worry about the little guy on your arm, he's filtering toxins from your system and is completely harmless."

As the immediate discomfort faded, Rafen's curiosity grew. "Where am I? Who are you people?" His voice was hoarse and quiet.

Shanice pulled a chair up beside the bed and sat down, her gaze meeting his. "You're aboard Star, she's a living spaceship. We—my crew and I—are what you might call... survivors. We all come from different corners of the galaxy. It's ok, we don't mean you any harm."

Rafen's eyes widened as he processed her words. "Survivors?" he echoed, a flicker of hope igniting in his chest. "Then, you're not with the Divinium?"

Shanice shook her head. "No, we're not. We've had our own run-ins with them, though. We found you based on a signal—well, it's a long story. But what matters now is that you're here, and you're safe."

A million questions raced through Rafen's mind, each one fighting for precedence. "And the others?" he finally asked. "The crew of the ship I was on?"

Shanice's expression hardened slightly, and she placed a reassuring hand on his. "They're gone, Rafen. Dead. But we managed to rescue you. It looks like you have been in pretty rough shape for quite some time. But that's all over now."

"Good." The young man replied. A conflicted look briefly passed across his face.

The reality of his situation slowly sank in. Rafen was free, saved by strangers from a fate worse than death. A strange sense of relief came over him. Away from the Divinium, out of the cell that had been his world for so long.

“I want to understand,” Rafen said after a moment, his voice stronger now. “About you, about this ship, about everything. The worlds outside my cell. And I want to help, if I can. I may not be much, but I’m done being a prisoner. I want to DO something. Anything.”

Shanice smiled, a genuine warmth reaching her eyes. “We have a lot to talk about, Rafen. And yes, we could use your help. But first, you need to rest, to heal. We’ll be here when you’re ready.”

"Why did you help me?" His eyes narrowed slightly, and he shifted his body away from her.

Shanice gave him the distance, she could tell that the young man was not used to kindness.

"Well, several reasons really. We were all captives ourselves until recently and know what it is like to be held against our will and tortured. Then Buddy vouched for you and said you weren't a threat. But mainly? Mainly it was just the right thing to do."

He took a moment to think about her response, but it had been so long since someone had shown him compassion that it was almost incomprehensible.

As Shanice stood to leave, Rafen caught her arm. “Thank you,” he said, the words filled with an emotion he couldn’t quite name. “For everything.”

Shanice nodded, squeezing his hand. “Someone else wants to say hello. I will leave you two alone.” She stood and left the room. He heard a brief exchange in the corridor before a strange object floated into the room.

Rafen shrank into his bed as the machine approached him, its gleaming body resembling two squashed spheres stacked on top of each other, and a bright blue light emitted from its core. Dangling from the lower part of its body were an assortment of wicked looking metal arms with a variety of tools at each end. The machine stopped ominously and raised one of its arms towards him.

"Beep."

Understanding dawned on Rafen's face. "Buddy? Is that you?"

The little robot chirped eagerly in response and waved its arm around in the air.

"It's good to meet you properly. Sorry, you weren't exactly what I was expecting." He laughed, and it quickly turned into a coughing fit. "I'd get up and say hello properly, but as you can see, I am not there yet."

Buddy drifted forwards and lowered himself to Rafen's bedside, chirping softly.

"Yeah, she gave me something for the pain. She seems nice. I haven't met a girl before."

Buddy tilted his body sideways.

"No, you are right, I haven't met an exceptional robot either!"

Rafen coughed again as he felt the machine reach up and touch his forehead. A tingle ran through his head and down his spine. "Is that what it is? I knew there was something in there that changed me, but I didn't think it was tiny robots. Hah, if only the priests knew theat we are more abomination than prophet. Is this why you can talk in my head?"

The metal arm felt cool on his forehead, soothing him through his fever as Buddy communicated to him gently.

"It happened when I was much younger, at a temple our people visit at puberty. Theres these two pools of water and we all get baptised in them. Very rarely, someone comes out changed, with visions."

Another soft trill emerged from Buddy's chassis.

"War and destruction mostly. Sometimes I see other worlds or great machines. I know languages I have never heard spoken and songs I cannot sing with one mouth. Creatures that cannot possibly exist and the taste of things you could never eat. I remember what it is like to die in a thousand different ways and how to kill a thousand more." His eyes filled with tears as he looked at Buddy.

"I have flown countless ships amongst ever changing stars but in the end they all go dark. I have seen so much of everything, but never optimism until you spoke to me."

The robot stilled and his arm pressed against Rafen comfortingly.

“Thank you. I understand. Will you come back and visit me soon?”

Buddy withdrew his arm and burbled a soft response before exiting the room.

Rafen lay back against the pillow, the pain and exhaustion pulling him back towards sleep. But as he drifted off, it was with a sense of peace he hadn’t felt in years. He was among the stars, and for the first time in a long time, he dared to dream of hope.

2. DEBRIEFING

"OK Team. Give me the sit rep" Alex said as he paced in front of the table in the rec-room.

Sorah, J'Coub and Shanice looked at him blankly as Buddy hovered, furiously reshaping a console into form after form.

"Are the translators down, Star?" J'Coub asked. "Either that or Alex is making up stupid names for things again."

"He means situation report, it's an army thing." Shanice said.

"Effective. Shortening phrases is much quicker. I like it." Sorah nodded in appreciation.

J'Coub shook his head "Only if he tells us what it means first."

Alex raised his hands in surrender. "Fine! Can I get a situation report? Please."

Shanice mock saluted, a wry grin on her face, "He's recovering ok. Out of the danger zone at least. Mainly he needs plenty of rest and good food, but it will take time. My main worry is the Flexium in his head. Buddy took a look at it and freaked out. It's inside his brain and wound down his spinal column, but there's no design to it at all that we can work out."

She pulled up a diagnostic scan of Rafen on the display table. "Buddy wanted to fix it there and then, but it's so intertwined with his neurological structure, which I might add has literally grown around the Flexium over the years, it could be incredibly dangerous."

"Any idea what effect it is having in him?" J'Coub asked.

Shanice zoomed into a small area. "Not long term, but he seems to be able to communicate with Buddy directly and if you look at this tangle of Flexium here," She tapped the screen again. "based on the electrical activity in his brain he seems to be receiving some kind of signal. The problem is, we can't work out what kind of signal this is or where it originates from."

Star spoke from the wall. "I am confident that the signal is only being received by Rafen and that he is not transmitting a response. The power levels involved would be impossible for him to generate unaided."

"Good to know." Alex acknowledged

Shanice continued. "Aside from that, his mind is incredibly active when he is asleep or unconscious. I suspect this is because of the Flexium somehow, but I do not know enough about his race to know that for sure, it may be something inherent to the people of the Divinium."

"Speaking of The Imperium." J'Coub sniffed in disgust. "Any guesses why he seemed, well, nice? Not spouting hate and all that?"

Sorah straightened in her seat and pulled a serious face. "You are an abomination. You disgust me. Wah Wah Wah."

J'Coub sniggered. "Yes!"

Alex watched the good natured banter between his team and felt himself relax even more. "I suspect it is partly because even in an evil empire, people are different. I guess being locked away in a tiny room by your own people doesn't help much either."

"Well, until he's well enough to tell us more, all we can do is keep monitoring him." Shanice said as she turned the display off.

"Ok then." Alex turned towards the others. "So, where do we stand on everything else?"

Sorah took out her pad and sent an image to the table. "As you can see, we have begun moving the wrecked Divinium craft to the other side of the mega-structure. Buddy and the crabs have interred any bodies on the mausoleum moon and identified anything worth salvaging. We won't have to worry about food for a while."

"Have we scanned for trackers and disabled any comm systems?" He asked.

Sorah raised an eyebrow. "Naturally. It was the first thing we did. With the ships themselves hidden behind the sun, if the Divinium come back, they won't even know the wrecks are there unless they literally stumble over them."

Alex nodded appreciatively. "Excellent work. J'Coub, how are things in the city?"

"Theres no damage to the city, the dome has self repaired and no full breaches took place. I have done several more supply runs in the last 2 days and we have more Flexium than we know what to do with. We can start on some serious upgrades to Star whenever we are ready. In devastating news, none of the Divinium ships had any alcohol on board."

"Sad news indeed. Star, how goes the search for the other member of your species captured by the Vrexen?"

There was a moment's silence before Star replied. "I have calculated the last known location of the vessel based upon the Divinium's encounter with them, but they could have gone anywhere since then. We will need to thoroughly explore that area in space to pick up any trail."

Alex pinched the bridge of his nose at the sheer amount of challenges that lay ahead of them. The team had come so far and achieved the impossible, but somehow in a short space of time, they had found themselves in a war against two fronts, a high-profile rescue mission, guardians of a massive supply of an incredibly powerful substance and caretaker of a millennia old mega structure, the only surviving evidence of a long forgotten Armageddon.

"Ok gang, so we have about a million things to do as urgently as possible. Suggestions?"

There was silence around the table as the crew tried to work their way through the enormity of what lay ahead. Even Buddy stopped tinkering and stayed quiet.

"Star? You have been at this longer than the rest of us. What do you suggest?" Alex asked.

Star's voice was soft and contemplative. "I must admit I am biased in wanting to find another of my species and free them, but we cannot leave this place unprotected and we certainly must be more prepared. We have survived so far by as much luck as skill."

"Do we have any probes we can send out to start the search while we prepare?" J'Coub asked as he scrolled through his pad.

Star's response was quick. "I am not outfitted with any probes, although this would be ideal."

"Shame, that would have killed two birds with one stone." Shanice shook her head.

Suddenly Buddy whirred into life and excitedly brough up the holo display. An image of three cartoon avians appeared on the screen and a rock flew by taking all three of them out.

"Three birds with one stone? Go ahead, what's your idea?"

Shanice asked.

The image on the screen adjusted as Buddy whistled away to himself. Displayed before them was the hanger bay with the various crafts stored there. Schematics of each flashed by as they were listed at the side of the screen. 32 small ships in total were listed, 32 once Buddy discounted Alex's car and not including the larger Vrexen craft they had used before.

"I had no idea we had as many ships in the hanger." Sorah observed.

J'Coub leaned in. "There's mine, the blue one. I only flew it once."

Buddy adjusted the image once more until J'Coubs ship was the only one displayed. They watched in fascination as the image became a blueprint and a list of adjustments and upgrades appeared along with the calculated amount of Flexium they would need.

"Fascinating." Star acknowledged.

Alex couldn't help but agree. "A fleet of small, fast attack craft that can be remotely piloted. Genius idea Buddy. Not only can they function as remote probes, but they can be used to defend the mega structure AND Star."

"I like it." Shanice said. "But we also need to upgrade Star herself and I would like to go back to the city to see if we can find any built in defences to the mega structure we can activate. There HAS to be something, especially since the self-repair functionality is still going strong."

"With that amount of work to be done, I suggest we dock at the city anyway." Star suggested. "If I'm going to get a whole new set of clothes, I'd rather not do it when we are so exposed."

"Girl you are going to look like an icon!" Shanice joked.

The lights shimmered from Star's wall. "Yes, I am thinking of something silver and deadly."

Buddy trilled in response.

"Then let's dock and start work!" Alex smiled.

3. BUILDING AN ARMY

The city was just as peaceful as it has been before the attack and there was no sign of any damage to the beautiful buildings. Star had docked in the same area as before and was enjoying a thorough clean from an automated machine she had identified on their last visit. Arrayed on one of the huge landing pads beside the dock were the assortment of shuttles from Star's hangar lined up in rows of six.

J'Coub stormed away from his old shuttle with a look of fury on his face. "They took everything! My wine, my clothes, my art! What kind of monsters ARE the Vrexen?"

Sorah touched his shoulder firmly. "The kind that kidnap, torture and murder people and use them for spare parts."

"Yes yes, horrible, but to take my wine? That is just pure evil." He retorted.

Shanice walked by with an armful of supplies. "At least you have your shuttle back!"

"Eh, it's a rental. I can't imagine what the late fees are on that thing now." He sneered. "But the wine was already a vintage, with another 15 years added since my capture, it would have matured perfectly."

Shanice rolled her eyes at him. "Theres still tons of rooms on Star we haven't explored. Cheer up, you might still find it!"

J'Coub's scowl melted away. "Hmm. You don't need me for the upgrades do you? I think the crabs and I have some exploring to do!"

He trotted away back to Star with a spring in his step.

Sorah turned to Shanice. "That man has some strange priorities."

"I know. But it keeps him happy and gives us a bit of peace. Speaking of peace, I may go and see if Rafen would like a small walk in the city. I think the fresh air and greenery will do him good."

"Do you think its safe to let him out and walk alone with him?" Sorah, ever protective, asked.

Shanice smiled. "Yes. He seems like a good kid and he hates the Divinium as much as we do. But if you are concerned, don't be, he's still pretty weak."

"Ok, but contact me if anything goes wrong. Buddy and Alex are just going through the final designs for the shuttles and we want to get them finished before we start upgrading Star. If you keep your eye out for any clues on the city's defences, or even the mega structure itself, that would be helpful."

Shanice nodded. "Just keep those boys in line. If we let them, Buddy won't stop coming up with ideas and Alex will be too excited to stop him. Catch you soon."

As Shanice waved goodbye, Sorah turned to look at the makeshift engineering table that Buddy and Alex had set up. It was a simple holo table surrounded by crates of Flexium and other supplies from the ship. Buddy was circling the table looking at a design from various angles, his manipulator arms bent to look like he had his hands on something approximating hips.

Alex was leaning on the table, peering intently at the image as Sorah strode over. "Here are the last of the parts you needed. How are the designs going on?" She asked.

Alex waved in thanks, without taking his eyes off the screen. "It's going well! We have divided the ships into three different squadrons. Scout ships, these are fast, hyperspace capable ships with powerful sensor tech and stealth abilities. There will be eight of these in total, designed to get in and out of places fast and unnoticed. We'll finish these first and set them off to search for the other living ship."

Sorah whistled. "Pretty! Nice and sleek, I like them."

Alex grinned. "Squadron two are similar but designed as fast attack drone ships. We will keep six on board Star and ten will patrol the mega structure. They will have a rudimentary AI on board and will be trained to use the acceleration network and the structures design to their advantage. We are sacrificing the advanced stealth tech and sensor array for light armour and laser weaponry. Their AI will also be hyperlinked so they can act as a unit as well as individually. You will have overall command of them from your station on Star but they will also act autonomously."

"I love it when you give me new toys to play with."

Buddy let out a long low whistle and started chattering away.

"All right, all right, I'm getting there!" Alex said before changing the displayed blueprint to another. "This is squadron three. Six heavy attack fighters. These will have thick flexium armour designed to take a beating and self repair. Armed with Missiles, energy weapons and smaller versions of the rail guns on Star."

Sorah studied the blueprints and nodded approvingly. "What about the last two ships? There's two missing from the flock?"

"Good catch." Alex, was unsurprised she noticed. "One is a complete piece of crap, so we were thinking we might add stealth and a basic guidance system and use it for either boarding a craft, or to load it with explosives and turn it into a giant missile. A final option kind of thing."

Alex raised a final blueprint on the display. "This last one is a beast. It took up nearly a sixth of the hanger on its own. It's already hyperspace capable, decent armour and weapons and a ton of cargo space. It also has a fleet of repair and construction drones on board. So, apart from a few upgrades, we are keeping it as is. It might be handy for supply runs, or rescue missions. Shanice calls it Thunderbird Two and insists we paint it green."

"Earth reference?"

"Earth pop culture reference."

"I see. Grerk!"

"I'm sorry. Grerk? That didn't translate."

"Great Work. I am using your efficient way of blending words. Great Work. Grerk."

Alex stared at her, his cheeks going slightly red. "Oh. Um, Ok. Its only really used in battle, or when celebrities get married. But, um, nevermind, I don't see why not. Thanks!"

Buddy, was still fiddling with the designs, completely ignoring the two of them, lost in his work.

"Tell me more about this Flexium. It sounds almost magical." Sorah asked.

Alex leaned against the edge of the holo-table, gesturing for Sorah's attention. "Ah, it is amazing stuff, but not as magical as you think," he began, summoning a holographic model of a Flexium molecule. "Imagine this as the ultimate Swiss Army knife of materials. It's not just durable; it's practically indestructible under normal conditions."

Sorah leaned in closer as he continued. "It's stronger than anything we've known—steel, titanium, you name it. But that's just scratching the surface."

He manipulated the hologram, showing Flexium morphing into various shapes and forms. "Flexium is highly conductive, making it perfect for any electronic or power distribution systems we need. Plus, it's incredibly versatile. Need it to act like rubber? Done. Need it to be as transparent as glass? Also done."

"The real magic," Alex continued, shifting the hologram to show tiny machines, "is when you use it to make nanites or programmable matter. Then we can shape it however we want, and it will 'remember' those forms until we decide to change it. But if we find a form that works perfectly for a specific function, it can lock that in and keep it indefinitely."

Sorah's eyes widened in understanding. "So, it adapts but also stabilises based on our needs?"

"Exactly," Alex nodded. "It's like having a material that learns and grows with us. The possibilities are endless, from building to repairing, to upgrading Star and our fleet. However," he added, adopting a more serious tone, "its adaptability is also its limitation. We have to be careful with how it's programmed. A mistake in its initial shaping could lead to unintended consequences, given its 'memory' capability."

He paused, ensuring Sorah grasped the significance. "That's why Buddy freaked out about Rafen. Flexium intertwined with his neurology without a clear design—its uncharted territory for him."

Sorah nodded, absorbing the information. "So, the coating on our armour is literally flexible but remembers to harden on impact?"

"Right," Alex affirmed. "It was programmed to react instantaneously in conjunction with the sensors in our suits.

Such a basic utilisation, but life saving. Star says our suits alone would be worth a fortune. It's one reason we need to be so careful about others discovering the mega structure. This amount of Flexium could start wars."

"So how do we get it onto these ships?"

"The ships are the easy part, really. Buddy will use some of the Flexium and the materials you brought over along with whatever is already on the ships themselves to create the weapons and the sensors needed. Similar with the engine upgrades so that all the ships have the same specs. Then we just coat them in the armour and programme it how to behave." He gestured almost casually towards the waiting shuttles.

"Star will be the harder part as the things we are trying to do there are much more complicated. We will have to build Flexium hubs across her body that are wired into Omni and powered by the ship. Then we create some pre-set patterns that are thoroughly tested. That way we can not only have a tough armour coating, but actively create different weapons or tools on the fly."

"Any kind of weapon?" Sorah asked, her eyes lighting up?

Alex laughed. "Any weapon we know how to make, have enough power to run and have created as a pre-set design template, yes. We can't safely create new ones on the go."

"Grerk. Then lets get started shall we?"

Shanice walked slowly down the ramp, Rafen leaning on her arm. His steps were slow but steady. His long curly hair was freshly washed and trimmed and although pale, he looked much healthier than he had before. His purple eyes blinked in the light of the sun and he took a steadying breath.

"Are you ok?" Shanice asked gently.

"I haven't been outside in so long. I had forgotten what it is like. Everything just feels so big." He stared around in wonder at the vast docking area.

She smiled gently at him. "Just you wait until we get to the city itself. It is so beautiful and full of trees and plants. We won't go further than the plaza today, but I brought us some food and drink so we can rest and eat there before we come back."

"We don't have many plants on the Divinium homeworld and the planet I did my pilgrimage was mostly desert. The only time I have seen more than a few has been in my dreams." He closed his eyes briefly, enjoying the warmth on his face then nodded. "Ok, I think I am ready."

Shanice led Rafen past the waiting shuttles and they waved at Alex, Buddy and Sorah in the distance. "Can I meet the others properly later?" Rafen asked shyly. "It's already a lot to take in."

"I totally understand. They can be a bit full on, but I promise you they are all really nice. We can do that this afternoon if you feel up to it."

Rafen smiled, but it looked a bit forced. "It's stupid isn't it? For so long I craved being outside and dreaming of making friends, but now all I feel is scared and overwhelmed."

"Its not stupid at all. For all that you have been through, it's amazing you can even still function. I told you that me and the others were all captured by the Vrexen right? Well, I was luckier than the others, I had just been kept in stasis. Alex, J'Coub and Sorah were all tortured horribly. Star too, for hundreds of years." She paused for a moment and looked off into the distance. "We weren't expecting to find you on that ship, but I am so glad we did. There's no better group of people to find healing with and work out who you are outside of that cell."

Rafen's face trembled with emotion and Shanice could see a genuine smile trying to break free from the turmoil. "Come on Rafen, it's just through here."

They arrived at the plaza, a wide, open space surrounded by towering trees and buildings just behind, with a fountain at either side. The water cascaded down in sparkling torrents, catching the sunlight and throwing hazy rainbows into the air. Benches were regularly situated along the walls, and the area was lush with vegetation, ranging from small flowering bushes to towering trees, their leaves rustling softly in the breeze.

Shanice led Rafen to a bench near the fountain, where they sat down. She unpacked the food she had brought—a selection of fruits Rafen had never seen before, and a couple of sandwiches made from ingredients gathered from Star's supplies.

As they ate, Rafen's gaze kept drifting back to the fountain and the plants. "It's all so peaceful here," he remarked, "like the complete opposite of where I've come from. I can hardly believe places like this exist."

Shanice nodded, understanding the sentiment. "I know what you mean. When we first discovered this city, it was hard to grasp that something so serene could exist amidst all the chaos out there. But it's real, Rafen, and it's a reminder of what we're fighting to protect."

Rafen looked at her, a thoughtful expression on his face. "I've spent so much time surrounded by hate and violence, it's hard to remember that there's good in the universe too."

Shanice smiled at him warmly. "There's a lot of good out there, Rafen. Sometimes it's just a little harder to find. But I promise you, it's worth looking for."

They spent the next hour talking and eating, with Rafen asking more about Shanice's crew and their adventures. He listened intently, absorbing every detail, and Shanice could see a spark of curiosity and perhaps even excitement in his eyes—the prospect of a life beyond the confines of his past slowly dawning on him.

The excitement in his eyes dimmed suddenly and Rafen wen't still.

"Rafen? Are you ok?" Shanice asked concerned.

"Yeah. I will be. I really think I will be." He smiled a genuine smile, albeit briefly and took another bite of his sandwich.

4. STAR

Star revelled in the feeling of the cleaning system. It was a luxury she hadn't encountered before. Buddy had done a good job of maintaining her recently, but he had been focused on repairs and the Vrexen only performed perfunctory cleans when they needed to which meant that centuries of grime had built up on her.

A small army of drones worked steadily over her body using a combination of nanotechnology, high-pressure cleaning fluids, energy fields, and precision robotics to clean every nook and crevice of her hull. It reminded her of the small creatures that would follow her pod back when she was with her people, a symbiotic race that fed on the debris built up on their skin as they drifted through space.

They, like the ancestors of the crabs that had once cleaned the teeth in her maw, but had long since adapted to live within her scavenging the corridors and eventually becoming a vital part of her waste disposal system, were a sign of a life long since lost.

A brief echo of grief ran through her mind. She was so far removed from the creature she had once been she no longer really knew what she was. The Vrexen had stolen her, mutilated her and over time changed her. It was only really when Omni was created that her sentience had grown to what it was now. A strange gift of higher intelligence only to allow her to understand fully the cruelty and suffering they had writ on her.

What was she now?

Drones blasted away stubborn dirt with their high pressure fluid jets, careful not to cause any damage. Huge swathes of accumulated space dust fell away in chunks, collected to be recycled by other drones. More drones worked on her engine exhaust ports, slowly returning them to an almost new state.

The other ship crossed her mind again. Truth be told, she had hardly stopped thinking about it. Somewhere out there was another of her kind, one who had gone through exactly what she had gone through, one who was like her. Just like HER! Her bond with her new crew was something she had never dared to hope for and she already thought of them like family. They had shared so many experiences, in such a short space of time, but it wasn't the same.

Secretly she yearned to be understood, to find that connection with someone else of her kind. A flicker of guilt crossed her mind for feeling such a way, she had far more memories of her life since she was taken than she could really recall from before, so why was this so important to her?

She shivered as tiny nanites slowly swarmed over her hull cleaning and polishing out any minor imperfections as they went. The nanites' gentle touch reminded her of the caresses of her long-lost kin, moving with a precision and care that seemed almost affectionate. Each movement of the nanites not only cleansed her but seemed to soothe some deeper, unseen scars—the ones etched into her very being by years of servitude and pain.

As the cleaning process continued, Star allowed herself to drift into a state of contemplation. The vastness of space had always been her domain, yet for so long, it had felt like a prison. Now, as she sat docked in the ancient city, she felt a glimmer of hope. The city, with its automated systems still functioning after eons, was a testament to the resilience and ingenuity of those who had come before. It was a reminder that life, in all its forms, finds a way to endure and adapt.

Her sensors picked up the chatter of her crew as they went about their tasks, their voices a constant hum of activity and life. They had become her companions, her protectors, her family. They had given her a purpose beyond survival, a chance to be more than a weapon or a tool. Through their eyes, she had begun to see herself anew, not just as a ship or a creature, but as an individual with thoughts, desires, and dreams. They had made her laugh for the first time ever.

Yet, the thought of the other ship, another being like her, captured and tortured, called to her with a sense of urgency and kinship. She resolved to find it, to offer them the same chance at freedom and understanding she had been given. It would not be easy—the galaxy was vast, and the Vrexen were relentless in their pursuit. But with her crew by her side, Star felt a strength she had not known before.

She considered the implications of finding her kin. Would they accept her? After so long, would they even recognise what they were, or had the Vrexen stripped away their identity as they had tried with her? And what of her crew? Introducing another hopefully sentient ship into their lives would change the dynamic in ways she couldn't predict. But deep within her core, she knew it was a risk worth taking. For too long, she had been alone, adrift in the void. The possibility of finding someone who truly understood her was too precious to ignore.

As the cleaning drones finished their work and withdrew, Star felt rejuvenated, not just physically, but emotionally as well. She turned her sensors outward, scanning the stars with a new sense of purpose. She would find the other ship, her kin. Together, they would forge a new path, uncertain but full of possibilities.

For now, though, she focused on the immediate future. Her crew needed her, and she would be there for them, as they had been for her. Together, they would face whatever challenges lay ahead, navigating the dangers of the galaxy as a pseudo family. And in those quiet moments, when the stars shone bright, and the universe seemed to hold its breath, Star would dream of the day she would no longer be alone.

5. J'COUB GETS CRABS

J'Coub breathed a sigh of relief as he entered the docking bay. The ship had been distracted as he entered, rippling in pleasure at being cleaned and his walk up the ramp had been far from steady.

Not that he minded helping with the ships or exploring the city, he just needed some time alone, something quite rare on his home planet. Sometimes he thrived being around other people and other times he found it incredibly draining. Even on board Star he still shared a room with Alex for the time being. He had just finished clearing and repairing some of the individual quarters, decorating them had really scratched that creative itch and he couldn't wait to show everybody.

He smiled to himself and felt his shoulders relax as he walked down the corridors, breathing in the gentle ship air. Star was apparently also enjoying some time alone as she hadn't greeted him when he boarded, but he could hear her humming a soft, melancholy tune from the Bridge as he passed it.

J'Coub and the team had done a cursory exploration of the ship when they had done the initial repairs, exploring all the major areas as they went, but Star was huge. There were so many non-essential areas still to check out more thoroughly and even whole corridors that they had yet to even go down. He knew for a fact that the crabs often disappeared when they were not helping him so they must go somewhere.

That settled it. It was as good a place as any to start his search. Pulling up the information on his Visor, he queried Omni on the location of the crabs but the search came up blank. Had they gone on the crab equivalent of shore leave? J'Coub searched his history to see if he could find any previous occasions where he had searched for them and was again met with no results.

Strangely enough, they always appeared whenever he needed their help, and J'Coub was astonished to learn that the crew's previous internal scans had never picked up on the presence of these little creatures. It was quite possible that because of their symbiotic relationship with the ship; they were actually counted as part of her. He pondered the question in his head and decided to head for the cargo bay to see if any of them were around. His favourite, who he had nicknamed B'Ayala was usually there somewhere.

J'Coub's footsteps echoed lightly as he made his way toward the cargo bay, his curiosity growing with each step. The cargo bay, a sprawling space filled with supplies, his workshop, and the occasional piece of salvage from their adventures, always held a sense of possibility for him. It was here that he felt closest to the essence of their journey, surrounded by the tangible evidence of where they had been and what they had achieved. He was also quite fond of the mess.

As he entered the bay, the usual hum of activity and machinery was absent, replaced by a quieter, more sterile atmosphere. He paused, taking a moment to enjoy the tranquillity, a rare commodity aboard a spaceship bustling with the energies of its diverse crew.

Then, out of the corner of his eye, he spotted movement. A small, familiar shape scurried across the floor, disappearing behind a stack of crates. B'Ayala, or at least, he hoped it was. A smile crept onto J'Coub's face as he quietly made his way toward the crates, keen not to startle his little friend. Behind the crates was a small gap in the wall, barely noticeable if you weren't looking for it.

J'Coub crouched down, the dim lighting of the cargo bay casting long shadows that danced across the floor. The gap looked like just another imperfection in the ship's vast interior, a reminder of the battles and skirmishes Star had endured over the years. Yet, as J'Coub peered closer, he noticed something extraordinary: a faint trail of scratch marks leading into the darkness.

Curiosity piqued, J'Coub pressed forward, squeezing through the gap. The air grew cooler as he entered a narrow corridor he hadn't known existed. The walls were lined with pipes, cables and pulsing blood vessels, humming softly with the ship's lifeblood. He felt he had stumbled into Star's veins, a hidden artery that pulsed with quiet energy.

The corridor twisted and turned, leading him deeper into the ship's bowels. Dust particles danced in the beams of light that broke through the occasional vent, creating a serene, almost mystical path for him to follow. Occasionally B'Ayala would stop just for a second as if she were checking he was following and then scuttle off round a corner.

As he ventured further, the corridor opened into a larger chamber; the walls echoing with the distant sound of the ship's operations. Here, the infrastructure was older, a part of Star that all but its most ancient residents had forgotten. He couldn't even guess as to what part of her body he was in now.

Suddenly, a soft chittering filled the air, guiding J'Coub forward. He followed the sound, drawn by an innate sense of connection to these small, industrious creatures. The chittering grew louder, more animated, as if welcoming him to a secret enclave.

And then, he saw it: a vast open space, transformed by the crabs into a sprawling nest. The room was alive with activity, younger crabs were playing and exploring under the watchful eyes of their elders. The walls were adorned with intricate patterns carved by tiny claws, a seemingly meaningless set of patterns that had a chaotic beauty to them.

Peeking around the corner, J'Coub was greeted by a sight that warmed his tiny blue heart. There, nestled in a makeshift nest of scrap materials and soft fabrics, was a small community of the ship's crabs. But these weren't just any crabs; they were mostly young, their shells gleaming in the dim light, a testament to their recent moulting. Among them were a few larger crabs, their shells marked with the scars of time, moving slowly but with a certain dignity. These, he realized, were the elders of their little society, respected and cared for by the younger generation.

For a moment, J'Coub felt like an intruder, a voyeur into a private world. Yet, the crabs didn't seem to mind his presence. In fact, two younger ones scuttled over to him, their antennae waving gently as if in greeting. He crouched down, extending a hand, and allowed them to explore his fingers with curious pincers.

"B'Ayala, are you here?" J'Coub whispered, scanning the nest for his particular friend. A familiar crab, distinguished by a tiny notch on its right claw, emerged from the shadows and made its way toward him. Its movements were confident, almost proud, as it climbed onto his shoulder and settled there comfortably.

J'Coub chuckled softly, the sound echoing gently in the cargo bay. "I found you. Or did you find me?" he mused aloud. It was clear now that this space, hidden away from the hustle and bustle of daily life aboard Star, was their home. A place where the crabs could raise their young, care for their elders, and exist in symbiosis with the ship that was their home.

As he stood there, a crab perched contentedly on him, J'Coub realized he had stumbled upon something precious and with a sense of reverence he slowly headed back the way he came.

"Thank you B'Ayala." he whispered as he scratched her gently under her chin. "I'm exploring today my little one. That was very kind of you to show me your home. I'll pop you down here so you can go back to your family and I will see you later." He gently lowered her to the floor, and she wiggled her legs until she was safely on deck. Since she discovered the zero G effect in the gym, she was now obsessed with being up in the air and often came to him to be lifted up or swung around.

B'Ayala clicked her claw a few times and wandered away back toward the nest. J'Coub squeezed back through the tunnel until he was once again in the Cargo Bay. He briefly leaned against the table he had used to fabricate the suit designs to think about where to go next. Pulling up his map again, he highlighted some areas that they had not yet fully explored.

Star was almost the size of one of the teardrop shaped skyscrapers in the city and that wasn't even including her tentacles. Sure, most of the space within her was taken up with huge areas dedicated to Omni, the power core, the shuttle bays etc and lots of her was still living tissue, but that left a lot of rooms.

J'Coub rubbed his brow ridge, a habit he often did when deep in thought, and marked some of the larger unexplored rooms. He would start in those and work his way down to the smaller ones.

J'Coub's curiosity led him down another series of winding

corridors, each turn revealing more of Star's hidden depths. As he moved, he couldn't help but marvel at how complex she was. Every inch of Star seemed to pulse with life and history and weird as fuck adaptations. The Vrexen had essentially mined into her body so her interior was more warren like than designed.

He approached a large, reinforced door marked with unfamiliar symbols towards the rear of the ship. J'Coub tapped a few commands into his Visor, attempting to decipher the markings. With a soft hiss, the door slid open, revealing a room unlike any he had seen before.

The first thing that hit him was the smell—a pungent, organic odour that made his nose wrinkle. The room was filled with machinery and vats of bubbling liquid. In the centre was a large, alien creature, its grotesque body a mass of writhing tendrils and gnashing teeth. The creature paused its movements as J'Coub entered, turning its many eyes toward him.

Tubes led down from various vats scattered around the room and he watched in awe as some crabs scuttled in along the high walkway carrying various bits of rubbish and organic material. They carefully deposited the waste into the vats and dashed away to find more. He watched in awe as the waste made its way down the tubes and into the creatures many mouths.

Fascinated, J'Coub watched as the creature chomped down on a piece of scrap metal, its powerful jaws reducing it to nothing in seconds. Another mouth sucked in a yellow liquid whose origin didn't bear thinking about. The creature fixed all its eyes on J'Coub and tensed, letting out a soft grunt as moments later, a small cube of pure metal emerged from its rear onto a small conveyor belt below it. It let out a small sigh and clear liquid emerged from what he hoped to the nine aunts was a tentacle towards its side.

Slowly the creature broke eye contact with him and continued eating. "Impressive I guess," J'Coub muttered, taking notes on his Visor. "Star really does have everything."

Leaving the Waste Recycler to its work, J'Coub continued his exploration. He soon found himself in a long, dimly lit corridor, the air growing colder as he moved forward. The walls were lined with what appeared to be personal belongings—clothing, trinkets, and small mementos. At the far end of the corridor, he found a room filled with shelves and display cases.

As he stepped inside, he realized what he was looking at: a Vrexen Trophy Room. Each item represented a life taken, a being stolen. J'Coub felt a chill run down his spine as he recognised some of the artifacts from paintings in his old gallery—items from races long extinct, their histories reduced to mere trophies for the Vrexen's amusement.

He moved slowly through the room, taking in the tragic remnants of countless lives. Among the items, he found a small, intricately carved figurine. Female in form but only loosely so, she held six orbs in her many arms. J'Coub carefully picked it up, feeling the weight of its history in his hands.

"Maybe we can find a way to honour these lost cultures," he whispered to himself, placing the figurine back on the shelf with a sense of reverence. His eye was drawn to a shelf to his left, there, nestled in between a strange helmet and a neatly folded item of clothing, was his crate of wine from his ship.

"Oh, my beautiful baby! You made it." He crooned as he picked up a bottle in his arms and rocked it slowly.

Caught in his reverie he almost dropped the bottle in shock as his comms crackled to life. "J'Coub, this is Sorah. You need to come to the dock. We've got something you need to see."

J'Coub's curiosity was piqued once more. "On my way," he

replied, making his way back through the winding corridors.

6. SHINY NEW TOYS

The upgraded shuttles glittered in the light. Despite the varied sizes and hull shapes, they were now all a uniform oily silver and J'Coub could recognise where sensor arrays and weapons had been fabricated and added to the ships.

"They look pretty!" He remarked casually as he leaned against the docking ramp. "You do realise we could all be decadently rich if we sold even just one of these?"

"How rich?" Alex couldn't help but ask.

Sorah kicked him in the shin abruptly. "I know you are teasing, but we cannot risk any of this Flexium getting into the hands of anyone else. Too dangerous by far." She huffed as she cleared up the last of her tools then paused. "How rich?"

J'Coub laughed at them. "Rich enough we could probably buy ourselves a small moon if we wanted to. But I totally agree, especially since both races we have met since we woke up have been total bastards."

Shanice and Rafen walked casually towards the group. Rafen still leaned on Shanice's arm for stability but the young man looked a lot perkier than he did before. He was wearing a simple blue jumpsuit which hung off his thin frame.

"Hi guys." Shanice said cheerily. "Look who is out and about?"

"Rafen! Good to see you up and walking." Alex stood away from the table and waved to the young man. "I'm Alex, the Captain of our little crew."

"Hello." Rafen mirrored the wave uncertainly. "Hey Buddy!" He turned and smiled at the little robot who bleeped happily in response.

Sorah strode forward confidently and clapped the young man on the shoulder, almost causing him to crash into Shanice. "Welcome to the tribe Rafen. You know who I am already, but I am in charge of security. You look like you will be fit enough to join us in the gymnasium soon enough!"

Rafen winced slightly and forced a smile. "I don't know what a gymnasium is I am afraid."

"Ah a man after my own heart!" J'Coub smirked as he sauntered from the ramp across to the group. "J'Coub. Information Officer, cook, art-dealer, man about town and anything else that's needed." He winked. "Anything..."

Rafen's skin turned slightly purple. "Thank you."

"Anyway!" Shanice rolled her eyes. "Are we ready to launch?" She gestured towards the scout ships lined up nearest to the dock.

Alex smiled and nodded "Yep, the scout ships are all ready to go. Star helped us plot in the destinations based on the data recovered, and we extrapolated some likely jump points in nearby systems, but, if the other ship has the same capabilities as Star they could really be anywhere. It's a starting point at least."

Sorah grinned. "Seeing as we are all here, shall we launch? I don't see any point in waiting..."

"Let's do it." You could see the excitement on Alex's face. "Buddy, do you want to take the honours?"

Buddy drifted over slowly and Beeped once. The designated scout craft all whirred into life as one, rising up from the dock.

"Oh, no ceremony then I guess." J'Coub observed wryly.

One by one the scout ships slowly manoeuvred out towards the docking bay and then moved out into the mega structure itself.

"They will enter the acceleration network one by one and then once well outside the hull they will each jump to their designated starting locations and begin reporting back. All we can do now is wait." Alex turned back to the team. "That and give Star her shiny new upgrades as well."

"Are you ready for your new outfit Baby Girl?" Shanice asked through the comms?

Star's voice echoed through their headsets. "Freshly showered and ready to get dressed!"

The heart of Star's upgrade lay in the newly constructed Flexium hubs that waited, ready on the dock. Like glistening nodes, they were going to be strategically placed throughout Star's framework, seamlessly integrating into her design.

Buddy, accompanied by Alex and Sorah, floated from one location to the next, placing the hubs and readying them for the synchronisation process. Each hub stood quiet for a moment and then slowly glowed as the connections formed with Omni.

Once the connection was complete, the nanites within the Flexium began to weave an intricate dance of construction and form, responding to the complex programming being fed by Star's computer network.

"You're witnessing history guys," Alex said, unable to keep the pride from his voice. He watched as a section of the hull shimmered and then solidified into a thicker, more robust structure. "This is more than an upgrade; it's evolution."

Sorah watched with rapt attention as the armour plating formed, its surface smooth and reflective one moment, then textured with intricate patterns the next. It was hard to believe that the ship beneath them was the same one they had once thought of as only a means of escape. Now, she was becoming their protector, their ally.

The first test of the weapons system was subtle, almost anticlimactic. A small turret extruded from the hull, formed from the same Flexium armour, its barrel glowing with contained energy. With a muted whine, it discharged a focused beam of light against a derelict piece of space debris, disintegrating it into a cloud of particles that twinkled like stardust.

Star's voice, modulated through the ship's intercom, was filled with a new undertone of strength. "Systems integration at 62%. Structural integrity increased. Weapon systems online. I feel...well, pretty fabulous to be honest."

The crew gathered, watching as more hubs activated, pulsing with a life of their own. Flexium's transformative nature was not just a shield, but a sword, a tool, and an extension of Star's will. With each pulse, the ship's potential grew exponentially, an armoured chrysalis preparing to unfold new wings.

Alex turned to Sorah, who was visually tracing the lines of a newly formed cannon. "Remember, it's not just the big guns! We now have the potential to adapt to any situation."

"Hey, you can't fault a girl for liking pretty guns." She replied.

As the last of the Flexium hubs activated, Star seemed to breathe deeply, her systems humming with newfound energy. "Upgrades complete. No issues to report. It will take some getting used to, but feels pretty intuitive."

The crew gathered in the central hub; the air buzzing with excitement and anticipation. J'Coub stood at the centre, a proud yet tired smile on his face. "Alright, everyone. Before we celebrate the upgrades and fleet I just wanted to let you know that I have selflessly been slaving away and the quarters are finally ready. Rafen's already moved into his room obviously, but now it's time for the rest of you to get settled in."

Shanice joked. "I hope you've made my room special, J'Coub. I have high standards."

J'Coub chuckled. "Don't worry, Shanice. I made sure each room has my personal touch. Speaking of which, I found something interesting during my explorations. There's a Vrexen Trophy Room onboard, filled with artifacts and belongings from their victims."

The room fell silent as the crew absorbed this information. Alex's expression hardened. "A Trophy Room? We need to document everything in there and see what we can find out about previous captives. Maybe even get word to some of their families."

Sorah nodded, her ears twitching. "Agreed. We'll deal with that after we get settled."

J'Coub waited for the penny to drop but couldn't contain himself. "Guys, OUR belongings were there. I put them in your rooms!"

With a sense of solemnity mixed with excitement, the crew made their way to their new quarters. J'Coub led the way, pointing out the details and modifications he had made to each room.

Alex's Room

Alex stepped into his room, it was spacious, with a large viewport overlooking the stars. A double bed dominated one corner with crisp, clean white bedding.

To one side there was a small desk with his old laptop, now suspiciously dotted with blue glowing circuitry, neatly placed in the middle. To the side was a small potted plant, and a carved magpie that once sat on his dashboard, one of the first pieces he had carved when he came home after his injury.

On a small shelf above him were a set of paperbacks that he had put into his car but never got around to taking to a charity shop and leant against them was his kindle, the reason for getting rid of the books.

On the bedside table was his phone, and a broken watch from his cars glove compartment.

He turned to J'Coub brimming with emotion. "You did a great job. This is perfect. That watch was my dad's, hasn't worked for years, but now it's the only thing I have left from him."

J'Coub nodded, satisfied. "Glad you like it, Alex. Need me to help test the bed?"

Alex snorted. "I'm not THAT grateful."

Sorah's Room

J'Coub led Sorah down the corridor to her new quarters, anticipation evident in his every step. "I think you're going to love this," he said, opening the door and stepping aside to let her enter first.

As Sorah stepped into the room, her ears flicked with amazement. The walls and ceiling were lined with warm, honey-coloured wood, creating a cosy, inviting atmosphere. Large windows allowed light to flood the room, and the view on the screens was of a peaceful, forested landscape.

The bed was a unique, round design, centred in the room and surrounded by lush greenery. The bedspread was a soft, mossy green, blending seamlessly with the plants that adorned every surface. Potted plants of all shapes and sizes lined the window sills, shelves, and even hung from the ceiling in macrame hangers. The air was filled with the fresh, earthy scent of the woods, making it feel like an indoor garden.

"This is incredible," Sorah breathed, taking in the vibrant greenery and the harmonious blend of natural elements. "It's like stepping into a forest."

J'Coub smiled, pleased with her reaction. "I knew you'd appreciate the plants. I wanted this space to feel more natural for you."

Sorah walked over to a small table where her personal items were carefully arranged. Her wooden box, intricately carved with symbols from her homeworld, sat prominently in the centre. Beside it was a small pouch filled with crystals and stones, each one carefully collected by her over the years. Leaning against the wall was her wooden staff, a symbol of her heritage and a tool she used in herding the young and lastly, her flute rested on a shelf, ready to fill the room with its soothing melodies.

"Thank you, J'Coub," Sorah said, her voice filled with gratitude. "You've outdone yourself. This is more than I could have imagined."

J'Coub nodded.

Sorah walked around the room, gently touching the plants. The shelves brimmed with different types of foliage, creating a lush, green environment. She could already imagine herself spending hours here, meditating, playing her flute, and tending to the plants.

"This place feels like home," Sorah said softly, turning to J'Coub with a smile. "I can't wait to settle in and make it my own."

J'Coub chuckled. "That's exactly what I hoped for. Enjoy your new room, Sorah. Try not to eat the walls!"

Shanice's Room

J'Coub stood outside the door to Shanice's new quarters, a proud smile on his face. "Alright, Shanice, ready to see your new space?"

Shanice grinned, excitement sparkling in her eyes. "Just open the door, J'Coub. I can't wait any longer!"

J'Coub opened the door, stepping aside to let Shanice enter first and her eyes widened in delight. The room was vibrant and cosy, a perfect reflection of her theatrical past and vibrant personality.

The walls were painted in a rich, deep plum colour and above the bed hung a large abstract painting with bold, colourful strokes, adding a touch of artistic flair to the room. "Wow, this is amazing," Shanice breathed, taking in the details.

"The bed is the centrepiece," J'Coub explained, pointing to the floral-patterned headboard. "It brings a touch of nature indoors." The bedspread was white, contrasting beautifully with the plum walls, and was accented with a deep red throw pillow and a mustard yellow blanket draped at the foot.

Shanice walked over to one of the bedside tables, where her bag sat. It was a stylish, over-the-shoulder design, and inside were her essentials: her phone, a purse, and a copy of "An Actor Prepares." Beside the bag lay her keys, attached to a keychain with a small photo of her mum. "You even found my book and keys," she said, her voice soft.

J'Coub nodded. "I wanted to make sure you had everything you needed. There's your yellow dress, too, I presume you wore it when you were taken." he said, pointing to the chair in the corner where the dress was neatly folded.

Shanice glanced at the chair and smiled. "It's perfect. Thanks, J."

Shanice moved to the floor-to-ceiling curtains in a light, airy fabric that allowed light to filter through, creating a soft glow. She pulled them back slightly to let more light in, revealing a large screen with an image of a field full of flowers. "The flowers are a nice touch," she said, her smile growing wider.

"I thought you might like them," J'Coub said, pleased with her reaction.

Shanice turned to J'Coub, her eyes shining. "You've outdone yourself. This is more than I could have imagined. It feels like home. Well, better than my crummy flat in Peckham, anyway. "

J'Coub chuckled. "I'm glad you like it. Hopefully it feels very YOU."

Shanice walked around the room, taking in every detail. The rich colours, the thoughtful decor, and the personal touches all combined to create an environment that was both stimulating and soothing. It was an ideal retreat aboard Star.

"Thank you, J'Coub," Shanice said, her voice filled with emotion.

J'Coub nodded, satisfied. "You're welcome, Shanice. Enjoy your new quarters."

As he left her room, closing the door behind him, Shanice sat on the edge of the bed, feeling a deep sense of comfort and belonging. Happy tears slowly slid down her cheeks.

J'Coub's Room

J'Coub stood outside the door to his new quarters, a mixture of pride and excitement evident on his face. He took a deep breath, savouring the moment before stepping inside.

As he crossed the threshold, he couldn't keep the grin off his face, after all, his room was naturally his masterpiece. The space was an opulent blend of art and luxury.

The walls were adorned with intricate bronze reliefs depicting scenes from various mythologies, adding a sense of grandeur and history to the room. Above the bed, a large, gilded frame held a stunning painting of the six brothers, commanding attention.

The bed itself was the centrepiece of the room, with a tufted purple headboard that added a regal touch. The bedding was luxurious, with layers of plush pillows and rich, golden fabrics. At the foot of the bed stood a beautifully crafted bench with an ornate wine rack underneath, filled with an impressive collection of wines.

J'Coub walked over to the side of the room where an elaborate bar area was set up. Shelves lined with bottles of fine wines and spirits, each one carefully selected from his personal collection and previously stored in his ship's hold, sparkled under the warm lighting.

Shelves and alcoves were filled with sculptures, vases, and other artifacts, creating a gallery-like atmosphere. Two plush, velvet chairs in deep burgundy with gilded frames were placed in one corner, inviting him to sit and enjoy a drink in comfort.

J'Coub took a moment to appreciate the atmosphere he had created. The rich colours, the luxurious fabrics, and the carefully curated collection of art and wine all combined to create a space that was very much HIM.

Feeling a deep sense of satisfaction, he moved to the plush chairs and sank into one of them, savouring the comfort and elegance of his new quarters. He reached for a bottle of wine, selected a glass, and poured himself a drink. As he sipped the rich, velvety liquid, he reflected on his journey and the memories each artifact held.

"This place feels like a sanctuary crossed with a gallery mixed with a brothel," he said softly, raising his glass in a silent toast to the future. "You've outdone yourself you handsome bastard."

7. LUNCH

"So, Rafen, what do you think of Star?" Alex asked as he tried to spear a small green sphere on his plate. The repetitive clink of the fork hitting the plate was making Sorah's eye twitch as the pea sized ball evaded him at every attempt.

Rafen sat awkwardly at the dining table in the observation lounge. He still wasn't used to being around people and was obviously doing his best to fit in. "She's Amazing. I have never seen something so beautiful in my life, visions or reality."

"He can stay." Star purred from the walls.

Rafen blushed a little at that. "I am honoured. Thank you, great ship. I am really enjoying getting to know you all. I am very curious about how many different species get along so well."

J'Coub casually interjected, "So, Sorah and I experimented with... well, interspecies curiosity." He rubbed a faint bruise on his arm with a smirk.

Shanice choked on her drink, sputtering as she set her cup down with wide eyes. "You what now?"

Alex's fork paused mid-air, an unspoken question etching his features.

Sorah shrugged, nonchalant as she plucked a bit of fur from

her sleeve. "It was a catastrophe. My horns aren't exactly... bed-friendly."

J'Coub chuckled, wincing slightly. "And Sorah's fur gets everywhere. I mean everywhere."

Sorah snorted. "And you, you're just too... smooth. It was like cuddling with a slippery eel."

Rafen looked between them, a puzzled frown creasing his brow. "Is this a normal bonding ritual I'm unaware of?"

Alex finally found his voice, though it was laced with disbelief. "You're both just... okay with this?"

Star chimed in with an amused chuckle, the lights on her walls flickering in a rhythm that reflected her amusement.

Shanice, finally regaining her composure, gave a nervous laugh. "Well, that's certainly one way to build crew rapport."

Sorah rolled her eyes, picking at her food. "It's fine, really. We're adults, we were curious, and now we know better."

J'Coub leaned back, his gaze flicking to Star. "I suppose you knew all along, didn't you?"

Star's voice echoed softly, her tone filled with a hint of mirth. "I am the ship. I am privy to all that occurs within my walls."

Rafen's frown deepened, still trying to catch up. "But... why was it terrible?"

J'Coub glanced at Sorah, and they shared a knowing look. "Let's just say our anatomies are not... compatible."

Sorah nodded in agreement. "And we have a much better relationship as crewmates and friends."

Shanice leaned forward, resting her chin on her hand. "So, no awkwardness?"

"Not at all," J'Coub confirmed, his eyes dancing with laughter.

Sorah added, "Why waste energy on embarrassment? It was an experience. A bad one, but just an experience."

Alex, finally managing to take a bite of his meal, conceded with a sigh. "Well, I guess it's good that you're both mature about it."

Rafen, still piecing it together, finally nodded slowly. "I don't understand why you had to touch bodies to get to know each other?"

The table erupted into a mix of laughter and groans. "They are talking about sex Rafen." Shanice gently explained.

"Oh. Okay."

Alex looked awkwardly around the room. "Sooooo, Um. The city was lovely today. Nice and, um, warm there isn't it?"

"Oh my god." Shanice groaned. "Are you THAT British that you are changing the subject to talk about the weather? In space?"

"Well, it IS nice. I like being outdoors, I used to go walking in the North Yorkshire Moors when my back wasn't too bad. I think after my accident, doing something like that made me feel a little more normal. I still miss it sometimes."

Rafen nodded. "I remember going outside a little when I was younger, but not much. My pilgrimage was the longest I ever spent under the sky and after that the elders walled into the ship. It's very strange being outside now, but I think I like it. "

Sorah chuckled, her tone lightening the mood. "My people mostly live outdoors. Our cities are open, built around the natural landscape. We only really spent time indoors for safety when the weather was dangerous or sometimes if the predators were hunting. We're creatures of the sky and plains, Rafen. Seeing the stars from a planet, feeling the wind—that's living."

Shanice joined in, a nostalgic gleam in her eye. "I used to spend sunny afternoons at Hampstead Heath back on Earth. Picnics on the grass, the city noise just a distant hum. I'd have a nice glass of wine in one hand and a book in the other, pure bliss. A jog around that park in spring felt amazing."

J'Coub made a face. "Outdoors is overrated unless it's a well-kept garden at a resort. Natural beauty is all well and good until you have to actually live in it. Give me a city with all the comforts any day. Countryside? Full of bugs and unpredictable weather. Not my idea of fun."

Star's voice resonated softly through the room, "I often wonder what it would be like to see a planet's surface from below its atmosphere. To watch clouds drift by, not just nebulae or the cold void of space."

Rafen turned his head, considering the sentiment. "What do clouds look like?"

"They're like cotton balls in the sky—sometimes light and fluffy, other times dark and ominous, full of rain," Shanice explained, her eyes distant with the memory.

"And they change," Alex added, "constantly moving, reshaping. It's so relaxing if you just sit and watch. I remember being a kid and talking with friends about what shapes we saw in them. It's kind of sad I stopped doing that when I grew older."

Sorah nodded solemnly, "On a clear night, we would look up at the stars and the moons, so beautiful. I used to think they were our ancestors watching over us."

"There's something poetic about you star-gazers," J'Coub quipped, "always finding the romance in the air—literally."

Sorah smiled, leaning back in her chair. "Maybe you need to spend more time looking up, J'Coub. There's a whole universe of beauty you're missing."

J'Coub grimaced. "Find me an artist to capture that beauty in a painting that I can hang on my wall and THEN I will appreciate it."

Alex chuckled at J'Coub's comment, "Speaking of families

watching over us, what were your families like? I grew up with just my mum and dad, but it was a full house with all the friends they would invite over."

Shanice's eyes sparkled with warmth as she responded, "Oh, my family was huge! Aunts, uncles, dozens of cousins... every weekend was madness. We'd gather for meals, and everyone pitched in. It felt like the house was alive with laughter and stories."

J'Coub nodded, a smile playing on his lips. "Different on my world. We don't have 'parents' in the same way. I was raised in a communal unit by multiple adults. Each one contributed to different parts of my upbringing—education, ethics, skills. It's more structured, less... chaotic than your Earth families, but it has its charm."

Sorah listened, then added her piece. "My family was my tribe. We lived closely with nature and each other, respecting the bonds we formed as sacred. We all had our parts to play, and it was often hard, but we also cherished our relationships. We could only survive as a unit."

The group's attention turned to Rafen, who had been quietly listening. He seemed hesitant, his voice soft as he began to speak. "I... I never met my mother. On my world, women are kept in enclaves, separate from the men. They say it maintains purity. Men take wives only when deemed worthy, and even then, it's rare."

He paused, swallowing hard before continuing, "Male children are taken at birth. Raised in the church, taught by the elder men. It's... I guess it's all I knew until I was taken."

A heavy silence fell over the group for a moment, each processing Rafen's words.

Shanice reached out, her expression softening. "That sounds

incredibly lonely, Rafen. Did you ever wonder about her?"

Rafen nodded slowly. "All the time. What she looked like, if she ever thought of me. But it's forbidden to ask, to even speak of the mothers. They are... almost mythic to us."

Sorah's hand found Rafen's shoulder, giving it a gentle squeeze. "You're with us now, Rafen. Here, you're free to think, to ask, to feel. You're part of this crew—your new family."

J'Coub added, "And in this family, we appreciate each other, regardless of where we come from or how we were raised. You're one of us now, Rafen."

Star's voice chimed in, echoing the sentiment with a warmth that resonated through the ship. "Indeed, Rafen. And sometimes, those families found along the journey are the ones that truly define us."

Buddy chimed in, speaking into everyone's comm units with a gentle beep.

Rafen smiled. "Thanks Buddy. Sorry, Uncle Buddy."

"It's incredible how you can understand him and have full conversations. Even though he could easily install a translator system, he refuses to do it for the rest of us, apart from Star. It's also incredible he want's you to call him Uncle Buddy. I KNEW he was a big softie." Alex teased, getting a rude raspberry sound over the comms.

"He's so nice, I like talking to him. He makes so much sense, not like Omni, they are REALLY hard to understand." Rafen pulled a face at the thought.

Shanice stared at him for a moment. "Wait. You can speak to Omni too?"

Star almost spoke over her. "I was not aware you could communicate with Omni, I have detected no interactions between you two."

Rafen looked worried. "I'm sorry, should I not speak to them?"

"No, no. It's just we didn't think that was possible! Omni is, well Omni is unusual." Sorah said quickly.

"Understatement!" J'Coub interrupted raising an eyebrow and continuing to eat his food.

Sorah continued. "It's a collection of minds from many different species, all wired together to work as a supercomputer. It's not supposed to have a personality."

Rafen shrugged. "Ok. That explains why it's so hard to understand. Sometimes it just makes big statement about stuff but other times it sounds different. Like it's sad, or confused. Maybe that's why I didn't think it was unusual to talk to it. I thought maybe that's just how AI's were."

Alex leaned forward, his interest piqued. "This could be important. If you can communicate with Omni in a way we haven't managed, it might help us understand more about the integrations they made to Star and their capabilities."

J'Coub scoffed lightly. "Or it could mean Rafen's got a knack for understanding confused, multiple personality computers. No offense to Omni."

"Omni says 'None taken." Rafen said, causing the whole team to eye the walls a bit warily.

Star's tone was curious as she spoke again. "Rafen, would you be willing to help us learn more about your conversations with Omni? It could be very beneficial for all of us."

Rafen nodded, a bit overwhelmed but clearly willing to help. "Of course, anything to help the crew. Wait, what's that noise?"

"Interesting you heard that just as I did as it was not audible. Everyone, we are receiving a signal from one of the scout ships we sent out." Star said urgently.

J'Coub looked shocked. "They found the other ship already?"

"If only that were the case. It appears to be a distress call from a small station orbiting one of the planets in a system called Vensag."

"A distress call?" Shanice asked. "From who? The Vrexen?"

Star transmitted the call to their visors. "According to the data packet I received, it is from a small mining and trading station populated by a variety of species. Their life support systems are degrading at an alarming rate because of a biologic agent which is slowly eating away at the insulation on wiring and other critical components, causing their systems to fail one by one."

Images of the bio-agent appeared on the screen, it's slow moving form reminded Alex of frogspawn, but much smaller. "The station's engineers have managed temporary patches, but the bio-agent keeps spreading, making a permanent fix with their available resources impossible. They are in an isolated position, do not have the expertise or equipment to resolve the issue. Additionally quarantine procedures have been activated meaning nobody on board can access their ships to escape."

Shanice grimaced. "That looks so much like chia pudding it's unreal. Star, based on the information they sent over do you know what this is and how we can counter it?"

"Indeed Shanice, according to Omni, it is Bravallian Fen Mould and I can replicate a counter agent to it quite simply."

Alex looked around the table. "SO team, who wants to be heroes and rescue some aliens that probably, possibly, might not want to kill us?"

There was a resounding yes, and the team sprang into action heading to the bridge to take up their stations. Rafen followed them cautiously, unsure of his role. "Hey, Uncle Buddy?" He asked over his mind link. "What is sex?" He cocked his head to the side. "Uncle Buddy? Why aren't you answering? Hello?

Hello? Oh, OK." Quietly, he walked into the Bridge wondering why Buddy insisted he ask Alex, the robot was usually happy to explain things to him.

8. DISTRESS CALL

The Bridge was positively buzzing as the crew cleared the exit from the mega-structure, the glow from Star's thrusters reflecting brightly on the hull. The crew had taken their stations on the Bridge with Rafen seated at the central viewing table and even Buddy had joined them, partially merging himself with the engineering station.

"We are outside of the Structure now. Star are you sure it's safe for us to translocate from here?" Alex checked.

"Indeed, once I am familiar with a location, I can open and close a portal easily. We only need to enter the outer system and travel back in if I do not have access to current map data. I will also use the data from the probe to arrive close to the mining station."

Shanice looked thoughtful. "Can we come up with a better name than 'The Structure?' at some point?"

J'Coub laughed. "As long as Alex doesn't pick the name, sure. But let's focus on helping these people out first."

Rolling his eyes, Alex nodded. "Star. Take us there."

"Yes Captain." Outside the ship, Star reached forward with her tentacles, each one glimmering silver with her new Flexium armour. Together they reached ahead of her and joined, the clubs forming a point.

The point pulsed with energy, a soft, luminescent glow enveloping the tentacles. Star's body hummed, the vibration carrying throughout the ship. The crew watched in awe as the tips of her tentacles vibrated faster, the air around them shimmering with a prismatic haze.

As the tentacles vibrated, they began to weave intricate patterns in the space before the ship, drawing lines of light that interconnected like threads of a cosmic web. The patterns grew more complex and dense, swirling around a central point that grew brighter with each passing second.

"Is she... is she creating a wormhole?" Rafen whispered, his voice a mixture of excitement and disbelief.

"More like a temporary rift," J'Coub explained, his eyes never leaving the spectacle outside the view port. "Her species can manipulate spacetime itself."

The light at the centre of the swirling patterns burst into a brilliant white glare, forcing the crew to shield their eyes. When they looked again, a tunnel of swirling colours and pulsating lights had formed, stretching out into the void.

"It's beautiful," Shanice murmured, her voice filled with wonder. "Like a bridge made of stars."

"Everyone hold on," Alex commanded, his voice steady despite the awe-inspiring view. "Star, whenever you're ready."

With a thrum that resonated through the very hull of the ship, Star propelled them forward. The ship entered the rift, and for a moment, everything went silent. There was a sense of weightlessness, a suspension in reality as they travelled through the tunnel Star had created. The walls of the rift glowed with an ethereal light, casting Star and her crew in hues of ghostly blues and greens.

Then, just as suddenly as it had begun, the sensation ended.

They emerged from the other end of the rift, the normal star-filled space greeting them. Ahead lay the mining and trading station, orbiting a remote, cloud covered planet. The station itself seemed peaceful from a distance, but the distress call had painted a different picture.

"Wow, Star, that was incredible," Rafen said, turning to where Star's presence was felt strongest.

"Thank you, Rafen," Star's voice echoed softly. "It's as Shanice would say, a pain in the arse, to do, but it is within my capabilities."

The ship approached the station slowly, allowing everyone to take in the view of the planet below and the station that now needed their help.

"Alright, team," Alex said, clapping his hands together as he turned from the view port. "Let's get ready to find out what's going on over there. Star, lets test your camouflage and see if we can pass as a regular ship for a bit."

"Acknowledged, Alex."

Star pulled her tentacles in close. Clasping them together at the rear of her body, she tightly coiled them in and around each other to form a bulging ring structure. As she did so, her hull shimmered as her natural mimicry abilities, augmented by her new Flexium coating, settled on a dull blue hull with the appearance of windows and external mechanics.

"Congratulations team, we have succeeded in making me less fabulous." She intoned dryly.

J'Coub chuckled at her. "I'm practically embarrassed to be aboard you. You don't stand out too much against that boring station, though, which was the goal."

The station resembled a giant spindle bulging out in the centre and tapering at the top and bottom. Three rings surrounded the main section, with windows uniformly spaced around their outer faces. The lower ring was clearly the docking area for the station and a variety of ships were attached to it. Their docking stations glowed red, indicating a locked seal to the station.

Alex took his position at the central console and activated the comms system. "Mining station, this is the research ship, Star. We received your distress signal and are here to assist. Please respond."

There was a brief pause, filled with static, before a voice crackled through the speakers. "Starship Star, this is Tamar Garel, overseer of the station. We direly need help. Our life support systems are failing. Theres a blasted bio-agent eating away at our wiring insulation. Goddess knows where it came from, as we have strict controls on that kind of thing. We've managed to slow the spread, but we can't fix it on our own."

"Understood, Overseer Garel," Alex replied. "We'll dock and assess the situation. Please prepare to guide us to the affected areas."

"Thank you, Star. We will await your arrival," Tamar said, relief evident in his voice. "Docking bay seven is clear for your arrival."

"You sounded dead professional there, Alex. Like you have done this a hundred times." Shanice pointed out to him.

Alex waved the praise away. "I HAVE Done it a hundred times, in my training memories at least!"

Once docked, the crew disembarked and were greeted by Tamar Garel, a tall, stern-looking man with a weary expression. His eyes, though tired, held a spark of determination. Trailing behind him was a younger man carrying two computer pads and a large cup. Both men were of different races, familiar from his memory implants. He immediately identified them as a Nxian and a Denerian.

Tamar, the Nxian, had a commanding presence with his dark blue skin that was patterned with intricate, bioluminescent markings pulsing subtly with his heartbeat. His eyes, deep-set and piercing violet, contributed to his air of authority and wisdom.

His hair, jet black and meticulously braided, fell to his shoulders, adding to his imposing appearance. Despite the weariness in his eyes, there was a resolute strength that made it clear he was a leader accustomed to hardship.

The younger man, clearly a Denerian, was in stark contrast to Tamar. He was shorter, with a lithe, almost wiry frame, and his skin had a pale, almost translucent quality, typical of his race. His eyes were large and bright green, filled with a mix of curiosity and wariness. His hair was short and silvery, giving him a youthful, almost ethereal appearance, which was ruined by the obvious stress on his face.

"Welcome aboard," Tamar said, extending a hand to Alex. "We are grateful for your assistance."

"Glad to help," Alex replied, shaking his hand, impressed at how universal the gesture seemed to be. "Show us where the problems are, and we'll get started."

Tamar led them through the station's corridors, explaining the situation. His squat torso rotated unnaturally as his long legs carried him forward. "The bio-agent looks like a rare parasitic organism that feeds on the electrical components crucial to our environmental controls. It's slowly eating away at the insulation on our wiring, causing systems to fail one by one. Our engineers have managed temporary patches, but the bio-agent keeps spreading. We don't have the resources or expertise to eradicate it completely and most ships refuse to dock to provide aid for fear of infection."

They arrived at the first affected area, a control room filled with flickering screens and exposed wires. The smell of burnt circuitry hung heavy in the air, and makeshift repairs lined the walls.

"This is just one of the many areas affected," Tamar said, gesturing to the damaged equipment. "We're running out of time and options."

Shanice stepped forward, examining the damage. "We can deal with this. I recognise it from our databases. Our ship can replicate a counter-agent to the organism. We also might be able to help repair and replace at least some of the damaged components."

"Thank you," Tamar said, his voice filled with gratitude and his antennae twitching. "I'll have my engineers assist in any way they can."

As Tamar called for his engineers, the crew began to set up their equipment. Shanice and Sorah focused on identifying and containing the bio-agent, using Star's advanced capabilities to create a counter-agent. J'Coub coordinated with the station's engineers, organising the repair and replacement of critical components. Alex oversaw the operation, ensuring everything ran smoothly.

"Alright, let's get to it," Alex said, his voice filled with determination.

Shanice and Sorah started analysing the bio-agent. "This stuff is nasty," Sorah commented, using her visor to magnify the stuff. "It's like a parasitic fungus. No wonder they couldn't handle it on their own."

"Yeah, but we've got Star," Shanice replied, injecting a sample into a device she had brought with her. "Star, can you analyse this and synthesise a counter-agent?"

"Already on it," Star responded. "It will take a few moments."

Meanwhile, J'Coub was busy coordinating the repairs with the station's engineers. He was approached by Hatteker, a gruff alien engineer who sauntered over casually, looking bored and uncertain.

"What exactly are you planning to do here?" Hatteker asked, arms crossed over his broad chest. His skin had a rocky texture, and his eyes glowed faintly.

"Apparently we are going to start replacing some of the damaged wiring and critical components, once the counter-agent to the virus thingy is dispersed" J'Coub explained. "It's a temporary fix, but it should hold until you can implement a more permanent solution. It will give you a couple of rotations grace at least."

Hatteker grunted, eyeing the equipment skeptically. "You better know what you're doing. This station is falling apart, and we're barely holding it together."

"Don't worry, we've dealt with worse," J'Coub replied with a confident grin. "Just keep your team ready to assist and show us to the bar once we are done."

As they worked, Hatteker peppered them with questions, his curiosity mingled with skepticism. "Your tech is weird. Is that biotech you are using?"

"It's a highly adaptable material we use," Sorah explained, not looking up from her work. "It is part tech and part biotech. Right now, we're using it to repair and reinforce the station's infrastructure where it will harden in place and behave in the same way as your original wiring. If you get worried, you can pull it out and replace it with your own tech once you have it."

Hatteker raised an eyebrow. "Sounds too good to be true. What's the catch?"

"No catch, just advanced tech," J'Coub replied, clearly enjoying the banter. "Also a bit of genius and a LOT of style, of course."

Hatteker snorted. "I'll believe it when I see it."

Rafen, assisting Shanice with the containment efforts, couldn't help but ask, "What kind of station is this, anyway? Seems like you've got a lot going on."

"It's a mining and trading post," Hatteker replied gruffly. "We handle a lot of different operations here, which is why this bio-agent is such a problem. We can't afford to shut down."

"Well, we'll make sure you don't have to," Shanice said, giving Rafen an encouraging nod. "How's that counter-agent coming, Star?"

"Just about ready," Star replied. "Distributing it now."

The team observed as they released the counter-agent into the affected areas. The bio-agent began to retract, its progress halted by the new compound.

"Nice work, Star," Alex said, his voice filled with pride. "Let's get those repairs finished."

Hours passed, and the crew made significant progress. The bio-agent was contained, and the critical systems were stabilised. The station's life support began to recover, the air growing fresher and the lights becoming more stable.

Tamar watched in awe as the crew worked tirelessly. "I don't know how to thank you," he said, his voice choked with emotion. "You've saved us."

"We're happy to help," Alex replied, smiling. "It's what we do."

As they packed up their equipment, Hatteker approached J'Coub once more. "I have to admit, you guys know your stuff."

J'Coub grinned. "No problem, Hatteker. Just doing our job. But hey, if you ever need more help, you know where to find us."

Hatteker nodded, a hint of a smile on his rugged face. "I'll keep that in mind."

With the immediate crisis averted, Tamar approached the crew with a grateful smile. "Before you head back, take some time to relax. The recreation section is full of people right now. Consider it our way of saying thanks."

"Sounds like a plan," Alex said, looking at his crew. "We could all use a break. Let's enjoy some downtime."

As they made their way to the recreation section, the crew marvelled at the transformation within the station. The lights were steady; the air smelled fresher, and the atmosphere was buzzing with life.

They entered a large, open area filled with various stalls and shops, vibrant alien traders selling everything from exotic foods to intricate trinkets. A lively bar at one end of the room emitted a welcoming glow, filled with the sounds of laughter and conversation.

"Welcome, heroes!" A booming voice called out. A rotund alien with bright orange skin and multiple arms waved them over. "I'm Gorak, the bartender. First round's on the house for the saviours of our station!"

The crew chuckled and approached the bar. Gorak served them colourful drinks in various glowing containers.

"Cheers!" Alex raised his glass. "To teamwork and new friends."

"Cheers!" the crew echoed, clinking their glasses together.

They found a table near the bar and settled in, enjoying the lively atmosphere. The crew members laughed and shared stories, the tension from the mission melting away.

J'Coub leaned back in his chair, eyeing the bustling market area. "I think I'll check out those stalls. Never know what treasures you might find."

"Good idea," Shanice said. "I'm curious about what kind of food they have here. Anyone want to join me?"

Rafen nodded eagerly. "I'll come with you. Everything here looks amazing."

Sorah grinned. "I'll stay here and monitor our stuff. Plus, someone has to keep Alex out of trouble."

Alex smirked. "As if I could ever get into trouble."

"Famous last words," Sorah retorted, rolling her eyes.

J'Coub and Shanice headed to the stalls, with Rafen trailing behind, his eyes wide with wonder. The market was a kaleidoscope of colours and scents, each stall offering something new and exciting.

At a stall filled with vibrant fabrics and clothing, J'Coub picked up a luxurious scarf. "How much for this?" he asked the alien vendor, a small creature with iridescent scales.

"Only 50 credits," the vendor chirped. "It's made from the finest silk on my home planet."

J'Coub haggled with the vendor, eventually getting the scarf for 30 credits. He wrapped it around his neck, striking a pose. "What do you think?"

"Very stylish," Shanice said, laughing. "Now help me pick out some snacks."

They approached a food stall run by a cheerful alien with multiple eyes and tentacles. The stall was filled with an array of alien delicacies, each more intriguing than the last.

"Try the Zoran fruit," the vendor suggested, handing Shanice a small, bright blue fruit. "It's sweet and tangy, perfect for a quick pick-me-up."

Shanice took a bite, and her eyes widened. "Wow, this is delicious! Rafen, try this."

Rafen took a bite and smiled. "This is amazing! So juicy!"

As they sampled different foods, they struck up conversations with the friendly traders, learning about their home planets and unique cultures. The experience was a delightful contrast to the usual tension and danger they faced.

Back at the bar, Alex and Sorah were deep in conversation with Gorak, the bartender.

"So, what brings you to this remote part of space?" Gorak asked, pouring another round of drinks.

"Long story," Alex said, taking a sip. "But let's just say we're explorers trying to do our part and help where we can."

"A noble cause," Gorak said, nodding. "It's rare to meet folks like you out here."

Sorah leaned in. "You must have some interesting stories yourself. Running a bar in a place like this can't be boring."

Gorak laughed heartily. "Oh, you wouldn't believe half of it. But hey, it's what makes life interesting."

As the night went on, the crew continued to enjoy their downtime. They mingled with the station's inhabitants, sharing stories, laughter, and a sense of camaraderie. The lively banter and friendly faces were a welcome change from the usual threats and challenges they faced.

J'Coub returned to the table, his arms laden with various trinkets and snacks. "Look what I found! This place is a treasure trove."

Shanice and Rafen followed, carrying plates of alien delicacies. "We brought snacks!" Shanice announced, placing the plates on the table.

"Perfect timing," Alex said, grinning. "Let's dig in."

The crew enjoyed the food, each dish offering a new and exciting flavour. The conversation flowed easily, filled with jokes, stories, and the occasional teasing.

"Who knew saving a station could be so much fun?" Rafen said, laughing.

"It's not always like this," Shanice replied, smiling. "But moments like these make it all worth it."

Sorah agreed. "And it was nice to meet some friendly faces for a change. It reminded me why we're doing this and didn't all just go our separate ways."

Alex raised his glass. "Great job, everyone. We handled the mission well and made some great connections. Let's keep up the good work and stay ready for whatever comes next."

J'Coub chugged a shot of his drink. "If it involves some cool stuff and delicious food. Can't complain about that."

As the evening drew to a close, the crew felt a renewed sense of camaraderie and purpose. They had not only saved a station, but had also made new friends and enjoyed a rare moment of peace and joy.

Suddenly, Buddy's cheerful beep interrupted the cosy scene over the comms.

The crew turned to Rafen, who just shrugged. "He says he's invited someone to join us, an old friend of his. He seems to be amused."

The crew exchanged puzzled looks. "An old friend? Who exactly did you invite, Buddy?" Alex asked, raising an eyebrow.

Before Buddy could respond, the doors to the central hub slid open with a hiss, and in walked a loud, brash figure lugging a large bag over his shoulder. He had unkempt hair, a scruffy ochre beard, and a noticeable swagger. His large frame was draped in a gaudy poncho that clashed with his green skin.

"Right then, where the bloody hell is Buddy? I've got a bone to pick with that bucket of bolts!" the newcomer shouted in what sounded to Alex and Shanice like a thick Welsh accent.

The crew stared in shock as the man dropped his bag with a thud and scanned the room. "Ah, there you are!" he pointed at the team. "Your mate owes me a pint, he does. Had me racing across the station for a bit of fun, did you?"

"Everyone, this is Li Davish," Rafen translated from Buddy's beeps. "He's a botanist and Mycologist. Buddy thought he'd be a valuable addition to our crew."

"A botanist?" Sorah asked, bewildered. "And why exactly do we need a botanist?"

Li Davish threw his head back and laughed. "Ah, you lot have no idea what you're missing! I hear this ship of yours is full of unusual plants, and that bio-fungus you lot encountered? I could've sorted that in my sleep if I hadn't been neck-deep in a barrel of Traxian Cider."

Alex sighed, rubbing his temples. "Buddy, why didn't you consult us before inviting him?"

Buddy beeped innocently.

"Li has unique expertise. Buddy thought he'd be helpful." Rafen said, embarrassed to be the go-between.

"Helpful? Bloody right I am," Li said, pulling a flask from his pocket and taking a swig. "So, where's this ship? And someone point me to the nearest greenhouse, will ya?"

Shanice couldn't help but chuckle. "Well, he's got spirit. I'll give him that."

Li grinned, extending a hand to Shanice. "Li Davish, at your service. And don't worry, I'm not always drunk. Just most of the time."

Shanice shook his hand, trying to hide her amusement. "Shanice. Welcome aboard, I guess."

Rafen stepped forward, curious. "So, you study plants and fungi?"

"That's right, lad," Li said, clapping Rafen on the back. "There's an entire universe of greenery out there, and I'm gonna find it all. Heard this ship has some unique specimens too. Can't wait to get my hands dirty."

J'Coub smirked. "Well, welcome to the team, Li. Just try not to blow anything up, alright?"

"No promises," Li said with a wink. "Now, who's gonna show me around?"

As the crew reluctantly accepted their new member and headed back to Star, Li strode ahead, dragging his overloaded bag and belching loudly.

"This should be interesting," Alex muttered. "That's two extra crew members we have, both found by Buddy. I'm supposed to be the Captain!"

The docking bay doors of Star slid open with a soft hiss, revealing the imposing figure of Li Davish as he stomped aboard, his bag slung over one shoulder and a flask clutched in his hand. He took a long swig, his eyes scanning the corridor with a mixture of curiosity and skepticism.

"Bloody hell, Buddy, where have you dragged me this time?" he muttered, his thick Welsh accent rolling off his tongue. "This better be worth it."

Buddy, hovering nearby, beeped cheerfully in response.

Li snorted. "I'll be the judge of that, mate."

As he walked further into the ship, his eyes widened in

amazement. The walls were not just metal and circuits; they pulsed with a bioluminescent glow, interwoven with vines and plant life. Strange, luminous flowers bloomed in alcoves, and the air was filled with the faint, fresh scent of greenery.

"Well, bugger me sideways," Li whispered, his usual brash demeanour softened by genuine awe. "This ship... she's alive!"

"Correct," Star's voice echoed through the corridor. "I am a hybrid of biological elements, advanced technology, and plant life. Welcome aboard, Li Davish."

Li ran his fingers along a section of the wall, feeling the warmth and subtle vibration beneath his touch. "Bloody fantastic. Seen nothing like this. This isn't just tech—it's a living, breathing organism. You can practically feel your heartbeat, Miss."

He moved deeper into the ship, passing through corridors where metal seamlessly blended with organic matter. Vines twisted around conduits, and strange, iridescent moss covered some surfaces, glowing softly.

"Look at this!" he exclaimed, stopping to examine a cluster of bioluminescent fungi growing in a corner. "I've spent my life studying plants and fungi, but this... this is something else entirely. A whole new level of integration. Fucking brilliant!"

Buddy beeped in agreement, clearly pleased with Li's reaction.

Li took another swig from his flask, shaking his head in disbelief. "You've outdone yourself, Buddy. This place is a bloody paradise for a botanist. Biological systems working in harmony with tech. And these plants! I'd sell my third bollock to have been the one that discovered even two of them."

He bent down to inspect the fungi closer, his eyes gleaming with excitement. "These beauties are thriving, right alongside the tech. Bloody hell, this is like finding the holy grail of botany."

Shanice approached, smiling at Li's enthusiasm. "Star's

integration of plants helps with everything from air filtration to structural integrity. It's a symbiotic relationship."

"Just be careful with that one," Sorah warned. "Some of those plants are... temperamental."

"Ha! Nothing I can't handle," Li said, waving her concerns away. "I've wrestled with sentient vines before. This is child's play."

Alex and Shanice watched from a distance, still trying to wrap their heads around Buddy's decision to invite Li.

"You think he'll fit in?" Shanice asked.

Alex shrugged. "He's definitely... different. But if he can handle himself and help us out, I suppose we can make it work."

"Star. Out of curiosity. How large a crew could you handle?" Shanice asked thoughtfully.

"With the various modifications The Vrexen made, I can comfortably accommodate a crew of 75, but maybe as many as 200 on a very temporary basis."

Li stood up, a wide grin spreading across his face. "Well, you lot have got yourselves one hell of a ship here. I'm in. Let's see what wonders we can uncover together."

"Welcome aboard, Li," Shanice said warmly. "We're glad to have you."

Li gave Buddy a hearty slap on the back, nearly knocking the little droid off balance. "Cheers, mate. Now, point me to the nearest greenhouse, will ya? I've got some exploring to do."

Buddy beeped and led the way, with Shanice accompanying them. Li continued to marvel at the living ship around him, muttering excitedly to himself about the endless possibilities.

The rest of the team stood aside, completely bemused.

9. HOME SWEET HOME

There was a strange atmosphere in the rec room. Everything suddenly felt so much louder than before. The crew were still adjusting to having Rafen aboard and now Li was sitting with them around the table regaling them with stories.

"I first met that bloody tin can when I was working on a Travarian Freighter. I got myself a job making sure that the seed bank they were transferring stayed disease free, and we had a batch of starter plants ready for transfer to one of their research stations. Course, he wasn't called Buddy back then. I just called him Rusty. He was, to all appearances, a cleaning bot on the ship."

Buddy swivelled towards Li and let out a low buzz, raising his welding attachment as if making a rude gesture.

The crew laughed, except for Alex, who raised an eyebrow. "So, Buddy was pretending to be a cleaning bot?"

"Pretending? He *was* a cleaning bot, did a bloody good job of it." Li said, taking a swig from his flask. "But I soon realised there was more to him. The way he moved, the way he seemed to understand things... So, I started chatting at him. One thing led to another, and we struck up a sort of friendship."

J'Coub, sitting across from Li, looked slightly grossed out as Li wiped his mouth with the back of his hand. "You... befriended a cleaning bot?"

"Why not?" Li said with a shrug. "Turned out to be the smartest decision I ever made, we kept in contact ever since. Rusty—er, Buddy—arranged for me to be in the area. Said Star needed a full crew to operate properly."

Alex sighed, clearly mildly annoyed. "Buddy, why didn't you tell us you were inviting someone new to the crew?"

Buddy responded with a series of beeps and whistles, trying to explain his logic. He spun in a little circle, beeping apologetically.

Alex rubbed his temples. "Alright, alright. Just next time, maybe run it by us first?"

Sorah, as usual, took things in her stride. She nodded thoughtfully, her eyes twinkling with amusement as she looked between Rafen and Li. "It seems Buddy has a knack for finding interesting people."

Shanice leaned forward, smiling warmly at Li. "Welcome aboard, Li. We're glad to have you. What made you decide to come along?"

Li grinned, reaching into his pack and pulling out a small container of seeds from the depths of the enormous bag. "Well, I've got these seeds here, see? I believe I can grow more plants that will be beneficial to Star. With her being a living ship and all, I reckon I can help her thrive."

"That's fascinating," Shanice said, her eyes lighting up. "What kind of plants are we talking about?"

"All sorts," Li replied enthusiastically. "Medicinal herbs, bioluminescent flowers to enhance the lighting, even some that can help with air purification. Star's already got a great setup, but I think I can make it even better."

J'Coub, still looking slightly disgusted, couldn't help but ask, "And you think those seeds will actually grow here?"

"Absolutely," Li said confidently. "Star's got an environment that can support all kinds of life. It's just a matter of finding the right balance. Plus, she's got a ton of fascinating flora that I haven't seen before. I can't wait to get cataloguing those beauties!"

Sorah nodded. "I like the sound of that. Anything to make our home better is a welcome addition."

Rafen, who had been quietly observing, spoke up. "So, you'll be working in the greenhouse, then?"

Li nodded. "That's the plan, lad. And don't worry, I'll clean up after myself." He winked, causing the crew to laugh again.

Alex leaned back in his chair, a small smile playing on his lips. "Alright, Li. Welcome to the team. Let's see what you and your plants can do."

"Cheers to that," Li said, raising his flask. "Here's to putting down roots and growing together."

Alex grinned. "Besides, if you think the plants on Star are cool, you wait until we show you the ancient city in the centre of an abandoned mega-structure. Full of extinct, thousands of year old plants if you are into that kind of thing."

Li choked on his booze, spluttering small drops across the table much to J'Coubs horror. "You what now, lad?"

"Li, we should probably bring you up to speed on where we are and what we're dealing with," Alex began.

Li nodded eagerly. "I'm all ears, mate."

Shanice pulled up a holographic display, showing a detailed map of the mega-structure and the city within it. "This is where we are based," she said, pointing to the central area of the map. "The mega-structure is massive, and the city is here. We have only explored a small fraction of it so far."

"It's like a bloody city on a ship inside a space station? A fucking massive one!" Li exclaimed, his eyes wide with amazement.

"Exactly," Shanice continued. "We've been exploring and mapping it out. The central area here," she pointed to a cluster of buildings, "is where most of the action happens. But there are vast areas around the city that seem to be fields. Nothing is planted there yet. We've been calling it the city, but we haven't settled on a proper name yet."

Li scratched his chin thoughtfully. "Well, if you're asking me, it looks like a bloody haven in the middle of all this chaos."

Shanice's eyes lit up. "Haven. I like that. What do you think, Alex?"

Alex nodded. "Haven it is. And for the entire mega-structure? We need a name for that too."

"How about Sanctuary?" Shanice suggested. "It's a place of refuge and safety."

"Sanctuary and Haven," Sorah said, testing the names. "I like it. It fits."

J'Coub groaned. "Corny!"

Star's voice resonated through the room. "Sanctuary and Haven. I approve. These names reflect the purpose these places now serve for us."

Li was grinning from ear to ear. "This is incredible. An entire city and a massive structure to explore and settle. What more could a man ask for?"

J'Coub chuckled. "Just wait until you see the places we've already found. There are areas filled with advanced tech, hidden chambers, and plenty of mysteries."

"Bloody hell, this place keeps getting better," Li said, shaking his head in disbelief. "What kind of plants have you found in here already?"

Sorah chimed in, "We've come across various bioluminescent plants, medicinal herbs, and even some that seem to have unique energy properties. With your expertise, we can cultivate and expand these findings."

Star's voice softened, reflecting her warmth and approval. "Having a larger crew and settling the city somewhat could be a wise idea. I feel we are going to need all the allies we can get."

Li's eyes gleamed with excitement. "I can't wait to get started. Imagine the gardens we could grow, the medicines we could develop, and the beauty we could bring to this place."

He looked thoughtful for a moment. "I know a few folks that may be interested. There's a group of people I used to work with who were setting up an Eco Sanctuary on a small planetoid. Seed banks, a selection of natural habitats for endangered plants etc. Even some small animals and insects. Bloody marvellous work, but the planetoid they bought was unstable and they are at risk of losing all their work. Mix of farmers, botanists, biologists and their families. They would be ideal if this city is anything like you describe."

Alex nodded, considering the proposal. “We need to verify their trustworthiness.”

Sorah agreed. "We can vet them thoroughly before bringing them here. Their skills would be invaluable, but we can't take any risks."

Li pulled out his communicator. "I can vouch for them 100%. Trust me, these folks only care about ecology. Somewhere secure and secret to work is exactly what they want. I'll reach out to them, but I'll make bloody sure they know not to yap about it."

As Li began drafting a message to his old friends, Alex turned to the rest of the crew. "We need to plan how to get them here safely. We could send Thunderbird 2 and the junk cargo ship, but that might draw too much attention."

J'Coub nodded. "Agreed. It would be safer to send encoded coordinates and meet them en route. We can guide them in properly from there."

Star's voice interjected. "I can encode the coordinates and ensure secure transmission. Meeting them en route would minimise the risk of revealing our location completely."

Li finished his message and sent it off. "Alright, message sent. They'll take a few days to respond, but I'm confident they'll be up for it."

Shanice smiled. "Great. Once we get confirmation, we plan."

"Most importantly, do any of them know how to grow Galbrothian Grapes? My supply is getting awfully low and we wouldn't want to run out of wine." J'Coub drummed his fingers on the table.

Li laughed and slapped the table so hard everyone jumped a little. "Mate! If there's one thing botanists are good for, it's brewing alcohol from almost anything. I have a feeling you will love them!"

"I have a suspicion you might be right."

Star spoke again, her voice urgent and shaken. "Pardon the interruption. One of our probes has sighted the other of my species. It is moving erratically, several systems from here. I have tasked the probe to remain in stealth mode and follow discreetly. I am putting some images it sent up on the display now."

The holo screen shimmered into being over the table.

At first, the images were murky and indistinct, a swirling mass of shadows and faint lights. The crew leaned in, trying to make sense of the chaotic display. Shapes flickered in and out of focus, creating a sense of unease and anticipation.

As the probe adjusted its sensors, the images clarified. Silhouettes of massive structures emerged from the darkness, slowly revealing the outline of a colossal ship. Their initial uncertainty gave way to a sense of awe and dread as the details became clearer.

The ship was unmistakably similar to Star, yet it dwarfed her in size and presence. Its hull was a dark, matte black, absorbing the faint starlight and blending almost seamlessly with the void. Unlike Star's elegant and organic curves, this ship was angular and menacing, built with a brutal efficiency that spoke of war and destruction.

Massive, reinforced plates covered its exterior, interspersed with rows of pulsating energy conduits that glowed a sinister red. These conduits traced intricate patterns across the ship's surface, reminiscent of a web designed to ensnare and annihilate. Weapons systems bristled from every angle—turrets, missile launchers, and energy cannons, all poised and ready to unleash devastation.

The ship's most striking feature was its array of tentacles, far more numerous and formidable than Star's. These appendages, armoured and armed, writhed with a life of their own, their tips crackling with raw energy. They seemed almost sentient, scanning their surroundings with a predatory intent.

As the probe captured closer images, the crew could see the ship's command centre—a massive, dome-like structure at its front. Darkened windows hinted at the sinister activity within, and the entire vessel exuded an aura of malevolent power.

J'Coub was the first to break the silence, his voice barely above a whisper. "It's like Star, but twisted... corrupted."

Sorah nodded, her expression grim. "This ship looks built for war. Whoever controls it has no intention of peace."

Rafen's eyes were wide with a mixture of fear and fascination. "Can we take it on?"

Alex stared at the images, his mind racing. "We need to know more about its capabilities and intentions. Star, can you keep the probe in stealth mode and gather more data?"

"Already done, Captain," Star replied. "The probe will continue to follow and observe. I will relay any new information as it comes in."

Li shook his head, still processing the sight before him. "Bloody hell, that's a monster. If it comes our way, I doubt we'll be able to face the bastard head on."

Shanice placed a reassuring hand on Li's shoulder. "We'll find a way. They don't know that Star is free of her Vrexen control. Maybe subterfuge would serve us better?."

Alex turned to the crew, his expression resolute. "We need to prepare for whatever comes next. This ship is a threat, but it's also a victim." He stopped and, despite the grim vision of the hulking warship, he turned to Shanice with a grin. "Shanice, when you said you were an actress, just how good were you?"

She looked him straight in the eye. "I got decent reviews when I had jobs, but I still mostly worked in call centres. Why?"

Alex stood up and headed towards the bridge, and Shanice stood to shout after him. "Alex. Why? Alexxxx!"

10. PLOTTING AND PLANNING

Shanice sat in front of the large display screen in Star's central hub, a sense of excitement mingled with nerves coursing through her veins. Her aspiring actress past was about to come in handy in a way she never could have imagined. The plan to board the other Vrexen ship required subterfuge, and she was the crew's best hope for pulling it off. That didn't mean she wasn't going to get payback on Alex later though. The sheer glee he had on his face when he suggested this was just a step too far.

"Okay, Shanice, you can do this," she muttered to herself, pulling up the video logs of the Vrexen that they had recovered from Omni.

The screen flickered to life, showing a series of recordings captured during the Vrexen's occupation of Star. The first log showed the Vrexen Captain, a towering, skeletal figure with dark grey, mottled skin and cold, black eyes. His puckered mouth smacked together as he spoke, and his voice was a low, guttural hiss.

Shanice watched intently, mimicking the Captain's movements and mannerisms. She paused the video and tried to replicate his deep, rasping voice. "Bring me a fresh specimen." she said, her voice sounding more like a croak than a hiss.

J'Coub entered the room, chuckling at her attempts. "Having fun?"

"Loads," Shanice replied, rolling her eyes. "This guy is a real piece of work. But hey, all the world's a stage, right?"

J'Coub ignored her strange idiom, his eyes twinkling with amusement. "Need any help?"

"Actually, yes," Shanice said, pulling up another log. "Watch how he interacts with his crew. There's a certain... disdain in his tone. I need to nail that."

"You could always imitate Sorah when she doesn't think we are picking up moves quick enough in training." J'Coub suggested.

They watched the video together; the Captain berating his subordinates with a mixture of contempt and irritation. Shanice paused the video again, standing up to practise. She straightened her posture, narrowing her eyes and clicking her tongue in a perfect imitation of the Captain's wet speech.

"You call this efficiency? You're all worthless! One of the test subjects would perform better than you, even after they were dissected!" Shanice barked, her voice a perfect match for the Vrexen Captain's harsh, guttural tone with the help of some voice modulation from Star.

J'Coub burst into laughter. "That's spot on! You've got the voice down. What about the body language?"

Shanice nodded, replaying the video to observe the Captain's movements. He had a slow, deliberate way of walking, almost like a lazy predator stalking its prey. She mimicked his gait, exaggerating her movements for effect.

"How's this?" she asked, striding across the room with a menacing air.

"Perfect," J'Coub said, clapping. "Now, let's see how you handle a conversation. I'll be one of the crew."

Shanice smirked, switching back into character. "You there, why haven't you completed your tasks? Do you wish to face the consequences of your incompetence?"

J'Coub cowered theatrically. "N-no, Captain! I-I'll get right on it!" His overacting was almost an art form in itself.

They both dissolved into laughter, the tension of the upcoming mission momentarily forgotten.

Alex entered the room, raising an eyebrow at the scene. "What's going on here?"

"Just perfecting my Vrexen impersonation," Shanice said, still grinning. "Think I can fool them?"

Alex nodded, impressed. "From what I overheard, absolutely. But we'll need to work on the disguise for sure! Star, can you help with that?"

"Of course," Star's voice echoed through the room. "I can alter Shanice's appearance using holographic technology and she is already using a voice modulation device. Calculations suggest that this will be undetectable by the other ship."

"Excellent," Shanice said, her excitement returning. "Let's do this."

Thin tendrils descended from the ceiling, weaving a shimmering holographic field around Shanice. Her features shifted, taking on the blank, imposing visage of the Vrexen Captain. Her skin darkened and became mottled, and her eyes turned pitch black.

Shanice looked at her reflection in the screen, her mouth dropping open in shock. "Bloody hell, Star, you outdid yourself."

J'Coub gave her a thumbs up. "You look terrifying. In a good way."

Shanice activated the voice modulation device, her voice now a perfect match for the Vrexen Captain's. "If you don't bring me a coffee immediately, I will remove your penis again!" she hissed, sending a shiver down J'Coub's spine.

"Alright," Alex said, clapping his hands together. "That is part one of the plan. Shanice, will initiate contact and persuade the Vrexen to allow us to board. The next thing to work out is how to take over the ship when we get there!"

"I'll keep watching the logs to understand as much as we can on how they interact and any interactions with other Vrexen. You guys go with Sorah to work on the next stage." Shanice slipped seamlessly back into character. "Let's give these Vrexen a performance they'll never forget you pathetic excuses for scientists!"

Star's bridge buzzed with activity. The images of the massive warship fresh in their minds, they were now gathered around the central table, discussing their next move. Alex, Sorah, and Star were leading the conversation, with Li and Rafen observing intently.

Alex began, his voice calm but firm. "Alright, everyone. We have a clear picture of what we're up against. This ship is a formidable threat, at least whilst the Vrexen are in control, but we have a plan. Step one is gaining entry."

Sorah nodded. "Shanice is our ticket inside. Hopefully, the impersonation works and we get docking access without trouble. Star, can we disguise your upgrades somehow?"

Star's voice was steady. "If I have to dress down, I suppose I will. I can project a convincing image of how I used to look and request docking. Once aboard, Shanice will need to maintain her cover while we prepare for phase two."

Alex continued, "Once on board we will need to act quickly. We need to subdue any Vrexen onboard as well as any security measures they have. We can't assume this ship is anything like Star inside, it looks like it has been adapted in a much more aggressive manner and primed for combat."

Sorah gestured towards the holo image. "We are going to need multiple safeguards in place and adapt as we go, with so many unknowns, we have to plan for any eventuality." She paused, a thoughtful expression on her face and her ears flicked upwards slightly. "Can we use some of the gas canisters Shanice came up with? Flood as much of the interior as we can with knockout gas?"

"The gas is effective in smaller enclosed spaces, but will not help us subdue the whole crew quickly and easily." Star said.

Li raised a hand, a thoughtful expression on his face. "Sorry, I know I am new on board and everything. But I might be able to help here. See, I have some beautiful little spores in my collection that would do exactly what you need. The Azure Nightcap has spores that will knock out anything smaller than a Zaladrillian Rhino and the Northern Creephold's are a fantastic paralytic. Some of those in a grenade combined with the Reacher Spores that spread like nothing you have ever seen before and yer Vrexen aren't causing any threats to you."

Sorah raised an eyebrow, impressed. "That could work. Bonus is it won't affect any of the captives in the suspension tubes. Do you have the spores?"

Li nodded. "I've got a few samples in my pack. With Miss Star's help, we can synthesise enough to fill gas canisters." He patted his stomach and belched loudly.

Alex smiled. "Um, Good thinking, Li. We'll use the spores to take out the Vrexen. Once they're down, we can move on to the third step: disabling the restraints and control mechanisms on the living ship."

Rafen leaned forward, his curiosity piqued. "How do we do that?"

Star's voice was calm and reassuring. "I can interface with the ship's systems remotely. Once you're aboard, I'll need to locate the central control node and get someone to disable the restraints. It won't be easy, but it's possible. Then it's just taking out any others one by one."

Alex continued, "While Star is working on that, we'll need to rescue any captives. They'll be in suspension tubes, just like we were. Our priority is to get them out safely. Sorah is finalising the details there. Li, Rafen as you guys don't have protective suits or knowledge downloads yet, it's best you stay on board Star and monitor from afar, we have no idea what's going to happen so we need you to be ready for anything."

"Does that mean we might get suits later?" Rafen almost bounced in his seat.

Alex smiled at the young man's enthusiasm. "Absolutely, you two are crew now! It might also be worth reviewing skill downloads with Star to see if there is anything compatible if you want it."

Li snorted. "Shanice told me about those. Feels like cheating somehow, I earned my degrees the old-fashioned way." He drummed his fingers on the table loudly as he looked around them. "Still, I'm not one to say no to new knowledge! Tricky part is picking only one. Shame it's limited to that. Ill need to come aboard anyway, but I will make sure I am safe. I understand the risks."

"Buddy isn't even sure it would work with me, what with the

Flexium in my head. Probably better not to even try, but I wanted one of those suits as soon as I came on board. They are SO. COOL!"

Star chuckled. "That's ok Rafen. I can set up a curriculum to your visor when you get one, you can learn normally."

As the whole crew gathered in the command centre for the final briefing, the weight of the upcoming mission hung in the air. The holographic display showed the detailed layout of the Vrexen warship, with various points of interest highlighted. Alex stood at the head of the table, his expression serious and determined.

"Alright, everyone," Alex began, his voice calm. "We're about to embark on one of the most dangerous missions we've ever faced. Our objective is clear: gain entry to the Vrexen warship, subdue the Vrexen, disable their control over the living ship, rescue any captives, and ensure the living ship is free and safe. Each of us has a critical role to play."

He pointed to the display, highlighting different sections of the ship. "Let's go over the plan and everyone's responsibilities one more time."

Alex took a deep breath and continued. "First, gaining entry. Shanice, this is where you come in."

Shanice, her Vrexen disguise already activated, nodded. "I'll use the holographic disguise and voice modulation to impersonate the Vrexen Captain. I'll initiate contact and persuade them to allow us to dock."

"Exactly," Alex affirmed. "Once we're aboard, Shanice will maintain her cover while we prepare for phase two."

He turned to Sorah. "Sorah, you'll lead the team to subdue the Vrexen and neutralise any internal security. You'll be using Li's weaponized mushroom spores to paralyse and sedate them. We need to move quickly and efficiently."

Sorah's ears flicked in acknowledgment. "Understood, Alex. We'll deploy the spores strategically to take down as many Vrexen as possible without causing collateral damage."

"Good," Alex said, turning to Star's holographic form. "Star, you'll be our eyes and ears inside the ship. Your job is to locate the central control node and guide Buddy and I so we can disable the restraints on the living ship. Can you handle that?"

"Absolutely, Captain," Star replied. "I will interface with their systems remotely and guide you to the control node." Buddy chirped in response.

Alex looked at Rafen, who was practically bouncing in his seat with anticipation. "Rafen, your role is crucial. Once we start freeing the captives, you'll guide them back to Star remotely. Only go in the ship if we are otherwise engaged and you absolutely have to. Make sure they're safe and secure."

Rafen nodded eagerly. "I won't let you down, Captain."

Alex then focused on Li. "Li, if you are insistent on coming, your spores are our secret weapon. You'll be guiding Sorah on where and when is best to deploy them. Once the Vrexen are down, assist with anything else that needs to be done and help Star with anything she needs."

Li grinned, stroking his pack of spores lovingly.

Alex took a moment to look around the room, meeting each crew member's eyes. "Remember, the success of this mission depends on our coordination and teamwork. We have contingencies in place, but we need to be adaptable. Trust each other and stay focused."

He pointed to the display again, highlighting the areas of interest. "We'll dock here, at the secondary hangar." His expression softened slightly. "We've faced incredible odds before, and we've always come out on top because we trust each other and work together. This mission is no different. Let's bring those captives home and ensure that living ship is free."

"Questions?" Alex asked, scanning the room.

Rafen raised a hand. "Have I got time to use the bathroom?"

Alex took a deep breath. "Yes, we will translocate in around 10 minutes, so everyone go do what they need to do. If there are no further questions, let's meet back here in 10 and prepare for departure. Let's do this."

11. INFILTRATION

"You know that when people spend so much time planning something out, everything is bound to go to shit, right?" Shanice joked wryly.

"Naturally! But when have we ever had a plan go super smoothly? Are you ready to give the performance of a lifetime?" Alex asked, a hint of a smile on his face.

Shanice grinned, her Vrexen disguise making the expression look sinister. "Born ready, Captain. Or at least 2 years of drama school ready."

"Then I think it is time you took the helm 'Captain'" Alec gestured towards the captain's chair. "I'll join the rest of the team in the rec room, but I'll be in your ear on comms if you need me."

As Alex left the Bridge, Shanice took a deep breath and spent a moment centring herself. She gripped the arms of the Captain's chair tightly and straightened her back. She let out the breath and spoke. "Ok Star, take us to their position."

"Yes Shanice. I am using the transponder on the other vessel to ensure we emerge from the rift as close as possible within standard Vrexen protocol. Initiating jump now."

As the rift in space grew, Shanice watched as she got her first closeup view of the larger ship. It was truly immense. Star slowly moved through the tear she had woven in space and as their field of vision widened, it was clear it was at least three times her size. Its skin was battle scarred, what little they could see, and almost completely covered in bulky technological enhancements.

Its surface was covered in thick armour that had been bolted across it, and spiked protrusions hinted at sensor arrays or weapons points, or possibly some kind of twisted Vrexen art. The panels themselves were marred with scorch marks and damage from countless battles, and Shanice had no doubt that this craft passed as a warship amongst the Vrexen.

Passing further through the rift, Shanice could see the huge tentacles trailing far behind the massive creature. Several were completely non-organic, indicating they had either been removed by the Vrexen or lost in battle and replaced at some point. Both organic and metallic tentacles bristled with spikes and weapons.

A chill ran down her spine at the sheer menace of the craft and she had to remind herself that underneath all the weaponry and armour was one of Star's people, a peaceful and simple race. The console in front of her started pinging as the Vrexen attempted to open communication with her.

Shanice took a deep, centring breath and accepted the hail. Instantly, a low, insistent voice echoed through the comms. "Vash, why are you intruding on my hunting grounds?"

Shanice's heart skipped a beat as the guttural voice of the Vrexen Commander filled the bridge. She forced herself to remain calm, gripping the armrests of the captain's chair so tightly that her knuckles turned white beneath her Vrexen disguise. The disguise was perfect, down to the mandibles that clicked menacingly with every subtle movement. But the real test was now — her ability to convince a fellow Vrexen that she belonged.

The Commander's voice crackled with suspicion, every syllable carrying an undercurrent of distrust. "Vash, answer me! Why are you here?"

Shanice took a moment, then replied in the deep, rasping tone she had practiced. "Commander, I am here under direct orders from High Command. Your prey is of interest to them, and I have been dispatched to assist in securing it and to deliver you a unique specimen."

There was a long pause, the silence stretching out painfully. Shanice could feel her heart pounding in her chest, the tension thick enough to cut with a knife. Every second felt like an eternity as she waited for the Commander's response. She could almost feel the suspicious gaze on the other side of the comms, scrutinising her every word, every inflection. It felt like the worst audition she had ever done.

"High Command, you say?" the Commander finally responded, skepticism dripping from his words. "And what interest does High Command have in my hunt? I have not received any such orders."

Shanice cursed internally, realising she had stepped into a minefield. "Well, shit," she muttered to herself, quickly catching her mistake before speaking into the comms again. "You know how High Command is, always keeping us in the dark until the last moment. They sent me as a precaution, should things get... complicated."

The Commander growled, a deep, rumbling sound that made Shanice's stomach twist. "Precaution? Complicated? Vash, you sound different... as though you have forgotten your place."

Shanice's mind raced. She needed to regain control of the situation, and fast. "It's been a while since I've had to deal with this level of incompetence, Commander. Maybe the stench of the underlings has rubbed off on me," she snapped, attempting to channel the Vrexen Captain's disdainful arrogance.

Another tense silence. Shanice could hear Star's systems humming quietly, the ship's presence a comforting reminder that she wasn't truly alone in this charade.

The Commander finally spoke again, his voice a low, threatening hiss. "Vash, this had better not be one of your famous schemes, or I will enjoy flaying the skin from your bones when you dock. I am allowing you to approach, but you will follow my orders explicitly. I'm curious about this 'unique' specimen you have."

"Of course, Commander," Shanice replied, her voice steady, though her pulse was racing. "I wouldn't dream of disobeying."

The comms went silent, and Shanice released a breath she didn't realise she had been holding. Her heart pounded in her chest, and she could feel sweat beginning to trickle down her spine. "That was close," she muttered under her breath.

"Shanice, you did well," Alex's voice came through her earpiece, calm and reassuring. "Stay focused. You've got this."

Shanice nodded to herself, drawing strength from Alex's confidence. She straightened her posture, letting the tension slip away as she focused on the task ahead. Star's holographic display lit up with the docking procedures. The massive Vrexen warship loomed even larger as they drew closer, its many scars and battle-worn exterior becoming more apparent. Shanice could feel the oppressive weight of its presence.

"Star, initiate docking protocols," she ordered, her voice back in the cold, calculating tone of a Vrexen Captain.

"Initiating," Star's calm, synthetic voice replied as the ship began aligning with the designated docking bay. Shanice watched intently as the massive docking arms extended, gripping Star with a mechanical precision that sent a shiver down her spine. She knew that every second was crucial, that one mistake could unravel all their plans.

As Star locked into place, the docking bay doors slowly closed, encasing them in darkness save for the dim, red emergency lights casting ominous shadows across the walls. Shanice felt a bead of sweat trickle down her temple, though her expression remained stoic beneath the holographic disguise.

“Commander, we are docked,” she announced, hoping her voice did not betray the anxiety she felt.

“Good,” the Commander’s voice crackled back. “Prepare to disembark and report to me directly. I want to see your face, Vash. I want to see what treachery might be hidden beneath it.”

Shanice swallowed hard, keeping her voice as even as possible. “Understood, Commander. I’ll be there shortly.”

As the comms cut off, Shanice exhaled slowly, forcing her hands to stop trembling. “Okay, team,” she whispered into the hidden mic, her voice barely audible. “Looks like it’s showtime.”

“You did great, Shanice,” Alex’s voice chimed in again, full of quiet encouragement. “Just stay in character, and we’ll handle the rest.”

“Let’s hope they’re not paying too much attention,” Shanice muttered, standing up from the captain’s chair. She took a deep breath, settling into the persona she had practiced so diligently. There was no room for error now. "Oh god, I need to pee so badly!"

As she made her way towards the docking hatch, the echo of her boots on the metal floor seemed deafening in the oppressive silence of the ship. She could feel the weight of the situation pressing down on her, but she refused to let it shake her resolve.

To her left, a specimen tank like the ones they all woke up in, hovered a few inches from the floor, the soft blue glow of its anti-grav illuminating the space and the shadowy figure within.

The hatch slid open with a hiss, revealing the dimly lit interior of the Vrexen warship. Shanice steeled herself, straightening her back and tilting her head upward in a show of confidence and authority. Every step she took felt deliberate, calculated, as she prepared to face the Commander in person.

With her heart pounding and every nerve on edge, Shanice stepped into the belly of the beast, the tank gently following her. The next few minutes would determine not just her fate, but that of her entire crew.

The Vrexen warship's interior was dimly lit, a harsh contrast to the sterile glow of Star's corridors. The air was thick, laden with the scent of oil, burning metal, and something more organic, more decayed. Shanice took it all in stride, maintaining her composure as she stepped forward with the specimen tank floating smoothly behind her. The glow from the tank cast eerie, flickering shadows on the walls, adding to the oppressive atmosphere.

She could hear the steady clank of Vrexen boots approaching long before she saw the Commander. His silhouette emerged from the darkness first—hulking, imposing, and bristling with the crude weaponry and armour that marked him as a seasoned warrior. His eyes, cold and calculating, scrutinised Shanice as she came to a stop a few paces in front of him.

The Commander's gaze drifted to the tank, and for a split second, Shanice panicked. But she kept her stance firm and her expression impassive, just as the real Vash would.

"Vash," the Commander greeted, though the skepticism in his tone was impossible to miss. "You have brought me this... specimen?" His mandibles clicked together in a way that Shanice knew indicated suspicion.

"Yes, Commander," Shanice replied, channelling the arrogance she had seen in the Vrexen Captain's recordings. "High Command believes it could be the key to unlocking the prey's secrets. They wanted it examined immediately by your scientists."

The Commander tilted his head, studying her with those unsettling, predator-like eyes. "And what makes it so valuable?" he asked, his voice low and dangerous.

Shanice felt a bead of sweat trickle down her back, but maintained her cool exterior. "Its composition is unique," she replied, carefully choosing her words. "It survived the destruction of several vessels in High Command's armada and showed resistance to our most potent bio-weapons. They believe it might hold the key to developing new, more powerful agents."

The Commander narrowed his eyes, but a flicker of interest passed through them. "Is that so?" he murmured, more to himself than to her. After a long moment, he nodded to the two Vrexen soldiers who had flanked him. "Take it to the lab. Ensure it is secured properly and that our best scientists are on it."

The soldiers approached the tank, and for a moment, Shanice feared they would notice something was off. But they simply activated their own anti-grav lifts, locking the tank into position and guiding it away down a side corridor. The dim light of the tank's glow slowly faded as they disappeared into the ship's depths.

Shanice exhaled silently, feeling a wave of relief wash over her. She wasn't out of danger yet, but the first major hurdle had been crossed.

"Come," the Commander said, turning on his heel. "We have much to discuss. You will brief me in person."

Shanice nodded and fell into step behind him, her mind racing. As they walked, she discretely activated the small, metallic strands that had been hidden within her uniform. With each step, they slipped out and silently integrated with the essential systems they passed—air circulation, security monitoring, and data relays. The tendrils were nearly invisible, and by the time they had connected, they were already fully integrated, unnoticed by anyone on the ship.

They reached the bridge, and the Commander strode to the central command station. The room was filled with the low hum of machines and the quiet chatter of other Vrexen, who immediately fell silent when they saw their commander enter. He gestured for Shanice to stand beside him as he took his seat.

"Tell me," he began, his voice still laced with suspicion. "How did you manage to intercept the prey? They have been elusive, to say the least."

Shanice inclined her head, carefully modulating her tone to match the Vrexen Captain's harshness. "I found them weak after their last encounter with one of our scouting parties. They are clever, but not clever enough to escape me. Their ship is damaged, limping along. I followed their trail, cornered them, and made sure they were within reach of your hunters."

The Commander grunted, his suspicions apparently mollified. "Excellent work, Vash. Perhaps you haven't lost your edge after all." He leaned back in his chair, a hint of amusement entering his voice. "You always did have a way of bringing the prey right where we needed them."

Shanice allowed herself a small, self-satisfied smile, keeping up the act. "I learned from the best, Commander."

He chuckled darkly, and for the first time since their

communication began, Shanice felt the tension in the room ease slightly. "High Command has been on edge lately, questioning the loyalty of even their most seasoned officers. I'll admit, when you first hailed, I had my doubts. But perhaps I was wrong to doubt your loyalty."

"You were right to question, Commander," Shanice replied smoothly, "but I assure you, my only goal is to see our science grow ever stronger."

The Commander nodded, seemingly satisfied, and a small silence fell over the bridge as the Vrexen crew continued their work. Shanice allowed herself to relax, just a fraction. She had him convinced, at least for now.

The lab was dimly lit, illuminated only by the soft, pulsing glow of the specimen tank that hovered in the centre of the room. Two Vrexen scientists, their eyes gleaming under the low light, hurried around the lab, their excitement palpable. This was no ordinary specimen—they could sense it. They had received many such specimens in the past, but none had come with such secrecy, such direct orders from the Commander himself. They approached the tank with a mixture of curiosity and greed, eager to unveil the secrets it held.

"Look at this one," hissed the first scientist, his mandibles clicking together in anticipation. "I've never seen a containment unit like this before. The design, the technology—it's beyond anything our research teams have produced."

The second scientist, slightly taller with a more angular frame, tapped a claw against the tank's surface, watching the energy pulses ripple along its exterior. "There's something unusual about it. I can't detect any organic material inside. What do you think it could be? How did Vash get his sneaky hands on it?"

The first scientist sneered. "Whatever it is, it's about to make us very famous. Imagine the recognition we'll receive for dissecting this thing and unlocking its secrets."

He reached out and activated a series of controls on a nearby console, attempting to access the tank's interior. The tank hummed in response, but remained sealed tight. The scientist frowned, his excitement giving way to frustration. He tried again, this time inputting a higher-level access code. The tank remained obstinately closed.

"Perhaps it's a new type of containment," the second scientist suggested, leaning closer. "Maybe the internal mechanisms require a more... forceful approach."

The first scientist, irritated by the tank's refusal to yield, slammed his fist against its surface. When it didn't open, he growled in frustration and kicked it, sending a resounding clang through the lab. The tank emitted a small, almost indignant "Boop," followed by a rude, mechanical sound sounded like an electronic fart.

Both scientists stared at the tank in confusion, their earlier excitement quickly souring into confusion and irritation.

"What kind of device is this?" the first scientist spat, stepping back. "It's as if—"

Before he could finish, the tank began to shimmer, its surface shifting and warping as if it were made of liquid metal. The energy pulses along the tank grew stronger, rippling outwards in waves, before the entire structure seemed to melt and reshape itself.

"Impossible!" the second scientist gasped, taking a step back as the tank began to shrink and reform into something completely different.

Within seconds, the containment unit had vanished, replaced by a hovering being of shifting metal plates and wires—Buddy, in all his peculiar glory. His digital eye flickered to life, glowing a mischievous blue. Without warning, Buddy gave a loud mechanical snort and unceremoniously dropped a figure onto the floor. Alex tumbled out, landing in a crouch before rising swiftly to his feet.

The Vrexen scientists barely had time to react before Buddy's manipulators shot out, gripping the first scientist with lightning speed. The scientist struggled, clicking and hissing in panic, but Buddy's grip was unyielding.

Alex, already in motion, darted toward the second scientist, who was scrambling to reach the alarm panel. With a quick, fluid movement, Alex grabbed the Vrexen by the arm and twisted, sending the scientist crashing to the ground. A well-placed punch to the jaw and shock from his suit glove knocked him unconscious before he could make another sound.

The first scientist let out a strangled cry, but Buddy's grip tightened, cutting it short and another arm with a syringe attached shot out.. A moment later, the scientist collapsed, subdued but alive. Buddy retracted his manipulators, the metallic plates of his body shifting and clicking into place as he turned to face Alex.

Buddy beeped, the mechanical tone carrying a hint of amusement as he raised a replicated thumb at Alex.

Alex, catching his breath, gave Buddy a quick nod of approval. "That WAS fun. Nice work. Let's not get too comfortable, though. We're on a tight schedule."

Together, they moved quickly to secure the lab, binding the unconscious Vrexen and ensuring the room was locked down. Alex activated a control panel on the wall, initiating a systems scan of the ship's core. The display lit up with a complex array of Vrexen symbols and readouts, indicating the presence of the ship's central AI—their version of Omni.

“Looks like their core is just ahead,” Alex said, his voice low and focused. “We need to access it and prepare the system for Sorah and Li. Once we take control, they can flood the ship with spores.”

Buddy beeped in agreement and transformed his arm into a sophisticated interface tool, plugging into the lab’s main console. The digital display flickered and then shifted, giving Alex a view of the ship’s internal systems. It was a mess of chaotic, overlapping codes—brutal and inelegant, much like the Vrexen themselves.

“Can you get us in?” Alex asked, watching as Buddy’s interface hummed with activity.

Buddy swivelled his head to stare blankly at Alex.

"Fine, fine, of course you can get in." Alex raised his hands in defeat. "I can’t believe I just got eye rolled by an AI."

Buddy turned back to the core and let out a low hum. He twitched slightly and data appeared on Alex’s visor. “Their system is primitive, by comparison. But there’s something... odd here. The AI seems... sentient, but fragmented. It’s like it’s been damaged, or repurposed.” Alex said, looking at the report.

“Hmm.” Alex muttered, thinking back to what they knew about how the Vrexen treated their own living ships. “The core might be a corrupted version of what Omni once was. That means we’ll need to be careful. If it detects what we’re doing too early, it might try to override or fight back.”

Buddy’s interface hummed as he continued to work.

As Buddy worked, Alex positioned himself near the entrance to the core room. His nerves were taut, every sense on high alert as they prepared for the next phase of the plan.

After what felt like an eternity, Buddy finally disconnected from the console. “Beep” he announced as a green thumbs up appeared on his screen.

Alex activated his comms, his voice steady despite the tension. “Shanice, we’re ready on our end. The AI’s defences are down, and the system is ready for spore dispersal. Tell Sorah and Li to get into position. It’s time to move to phase two.”

A moment later, Shanice’s voice came through, calm and composed. “Copy that, Alex. I’ve got the Commander occupied. We’ll have the spores ready to disperse as soon as you give the signal.”

“Roger that,” Alex replied, glancing at Buddy, who was already transforming one of his appendages into a high-powered emitter for the spores that he carried. “We’re heading to environmental now. Let’s finish this.”

12. PHASE 2

Sorah and Li

Sorah moved through the dimly lit corridors of the Vrexen warship with the silent precision of a predator, the memory of being prey herself long forgotten. Li, following close behind, clutched a small canister containing the spores that would soon be released into the ship's ventilation system. He wore a hazmat suit that he often used when working around dangerous plants, but still had his ridiculous poncho draped over the top.

They had docked one of the small shuttles on the far side of the ship, away from the bridge, and had managed to slip past the initial patrols thanks to Shanice's distraction and the filament disruptors she had subtly deployed.

As they approached the entrance to the environmental control chamber, Sorah signalled for Li to stay back. She could hear the faint, guttural voices of Vrexen guards stationed just beyond the next bulkhead. Her ears twitched as she listened intently, counting at least three distinct voices.

Without a word, Sorah unsheathed her suits twin blades, the metal gleaming in the low light. She moved like a shadow, her feet barely making a sound on the metal floor. The door to the chamber was slightly ajar, and she slipped inside, pressing her back against the wall as she surveyed the scene.

Three Vrexen guards stood near the central console, their attention focused on a holographic display. Sorah's muscles tensed, and in one fluid motion, she lunged forward. The first guard didn't even have time to react as her blade sliced through the air, severing his communication link and silencing his voice forever. The second guard turned just in time to see the glint of her blade before it buried itself in his throat.

The third guard reached for his weapon, but Sorah was faster. She spun around, using her momentum to bring her second blade across his chest in a deadly arc. The guard crumpled to the ground, a gurgled gasp escaping his lips as life drained from his eyes.

"Clear," Sorah whispered into her comms, barely out of breath.

Li quickly entered the room, eyes wide with a mix of awe and relief. "Remind me never to get on your bad side," he muttered as he moved to the environmental control panel.

Sorah allowed herself a brief smile before turning serious again. "Just get the spores into the system. We're on a tight schedule."

Li nodded, his hands moving swiftly as he accessed the ship's ventilation controls. He inserted the canister into the system, and with a press of a button, the spores were released. They would spread quickly through the ship, taking down the Vrexen soldiers and leaving the captives unharmed in their suspension tubes.

"Done," Li whispered, sealing the canister and stepping back. "The spores should reach the critical areas within minutes."

Sorah activated her comms, signalling the others. "Spores are in the system. Proceeding to phase two."

Alex and Buddy

Deep within the bowels of the ship, Alex and Buddy moved through the narrow corridors, their path illuminated by the faint glow of Buddy's shifting form. They reached the access point to the ship's environmental systems, where Buddy immediately plugged into the control panel.

"How's it looking?" Alex asked, keeping his eyes on the surrounding area.

"Beep," Buddy replied, his voice calm as his tendrils worked their way into the ship's systems. A series of green tick appeared on his screen.

"Good," Alex said, his grip tightening on his weapon.

"Once those spores are in play, we need to move fast. We can't let any of them have time to react."

Buddy beeped in agreement as he finished the final connection and again have a thumbs up

Alex nodded and spoke into his comms. "Spores are dispersing now. Let's make sure they don't have a chance to call for reinforcements."

As they moved toward the ship's core, the effect of Shanice's filaments became evident. The internal communications of the Vrexen warship were already beginning to falter, with lights flickering and terminals glitching as Star and J'Coub's hacking efforts bore fruit. Alex could hear the distorted, fragmented attempts at communication from the Vrexen crew over the ship's intercoms, their confusion and panic evident.

"J'Coub's doing good work," Alex murmured. "They're scrambling."

Shanice

Back on the bridge, Shanice was playing her role to perfection. She maintained her stoic, commanding presence, even as the Commander continued to question her about the mission details. Each moment of his distraction was a moment closer to their victory.

But time was running out, and she knew she had to act soon.

Casually, as if adjusting her uniform, Shanice tapped a hidden compartment on her belt. A small nozzle extended from the fabric, almost invisible to the naked eye. She moved closer to the central ventilation shaft that ran through the bridge, her movements calculated and precise.

The Commander continued to drone on about battle tactics, his confidence growing with each passing second. Shanice nodded at the appropriate moments, feigning interest, all while positioning herself near the ventilation system. With a subtle press of the nozzle, the spores were released into the air.

The effect was almost immediate. The Commander, mid-sentence, began to falter, his words slurring as his eyes drooped. One by one, the Vrexen bridge crew followed suit, their aggressive postures slackening as they succumbed to the spores. Shanice took a step back, watching as the powerful warriors crumpled to the ground, unconscious.

The Commander tried to rise, his mandibles clicking weakly as he struggled to maintain control. Shanice knelt beside him, her Vrexen disguise still perfectly in place, and whispered in his ear, "You should have trusted your instincts, Commander."

With that, he slumped to the floor, unconscious like the rest.

Quickly, Shanice moved to the command console, her fingers

flying over the controls as she began to hack into the ship's main systems. The filaments she had released earlier were already at work, disrupting communications and weakening security protocols, but she needed to ensure they had full control.

"Star, I'm in," she whispered into her comms. "Starting the unlocking procedure on the ship's restraints."

"Good work, Shanice," Star's voice responded, filled with a quiet intensity. "I'm coordinating with J'Coub. We're gaining control of their systems. They won't know what hit them."

But even as Star began to take over the Vrexen systems, a new presence made itself known. Deep within the warship, the other living ship—the one corrupted and enslaved by the Vrexen—began to stir. Star's voice, usually calm and measured, now held a note of desperation.

"I'm trying to reach him," she whispered, almost to herself. "He's there, underneath the programming. I just need to... please, listen to me. We're here to help."

The ship responded, its corrupted systems fighting back, but Star was relentless. Her voice echoed through the connection, a promise and a plea. "We can free you. Just hold on a little longer."

J'Coub and Star

Back on their own ship, J'Coub sat at the central console, his hands moving rapidly over the controls as he assisted Star in hacking the enemy systems. His brow was furrowed with concentration, the complexity of the task evident in every keystroke.

"Come on, Star," he muttered, his eyes locked on the data streams flooding the screen. "You've got this."

Star's voice, usually so confident, was filled with an edge of urgency. "He's in pain, J'Coub. They've twisted him, broken him... I can barely reach through the corruption."

"Don't give up," J'Coub urged, his fingers flying over the console as he tried to strengthen their connection. "We're close. Just keep talking to him."

"I won't stop," Star replied, her voice soft but resolute. "Not until he's free."

As J'Coub continued his work, he glanced at the tactical display. The ship's core was almost within reach, and once Alex and Buddy made it there, they could initiate the final phase.

"Almost there," J'Coub said, more to himself than anyone else. "Just a little longer."

Alex and Buddy

Alex and Buddy moved swiftly through the ship's core, the spores they had released earlier doing their work. Vrexen guards slumped against walls, unconscious, their weapons clattering to the floor. The deeper they went, the quieter it became, the sound of the ship's systems humming softly in the background.

They reached the core's main chamber, a massive, pulsing nexus of wires, conduits, and organic material. The enemy AI was housed here, its presence like a dark, twisted mirror of Star's own intelligence.

"Ready?" Alex asked, glancing at Buddy.

Buddy beeped affirmatively, his form shifting into a more

combat-ready stance.

Together, they approached the core. As they prepared to insert the final override, Alex activated his comms. "Sorah, Li—get ready. We're about to initiate the lockdown. Flood the rest of the ship with spores and make sure no one escapes."

"Understood," Sorah's voice came back, calm and focused. "We're in position. Ready when you are."

Alex exchanged a final look with Buddy before turning his attention to the core. "It's time to end this."

Shanice and Li

Shanice and Li moved quickly through the now-silent corridors of the Vrexen ship, their footsteps echoing off the metal floors. The spores had done their job, rendering the once-dangerous enemies unconscious, but the real work was just beginning. They reached the entrance to the ship's laboratory, a place that Shanice dreaded to enter but knew was necessary.

The lab doors slid open with a hiss, revealing rows upon rows of stasis tubes, each one containing a victim of the Vrexen's horrific experiments. The tubes were arranged in a cold, methodical manner, the soft blue light they emitted casting an eerie glow across the room.

Li stepped forward, his face set in grim determination. "We need to find out how many are here and get them out. Star can handle the transfer, but it's going to take time."

Shanice nodded, her stomach churning as she approached the nearest tube. The figure inside was barely recognisable, their features distorted and marred by the cruel surgeries and augmentations the Vrexen had inflicted. "This is... worse than I imagined," she whispered, placing a hand on the tube's surface.

Li activated a nearby console, pulling up the data on each of the stasis tubes. "Fifty," he said, his voice tight. "Fifty fucking captives, all from different races, all... altered."

Shanice took a deep breath, trying to steady herself. "We need to get them out of here. Star, can you begin the transfer process?"

Star's voice came through the comms, gentle and reassuring. "I'm ready, Shanice. I've already begun preparing the medical bay. The transfer will take some time, but I'll make sure each one is stable during transit."

"Good," Shanice replied, her resolve hardening. "We'll start with the ones in the worst condition."

Together, Shanice and Li began the painstaking process of transferring the captives. Each tube was carefully disengaged from the Vrexen systems, and moved onto the transport platforms that would carry them back to safety. The faces of the captives, twisted in pain even in their unconscious state, haunted Shanice as she worked. She couldn't help but wonder how many would even survive once they were freed.

Alex and Buddy

Meanwhile, Alex and Buddy were deep within the ship's core, working methodically to override more of the locks that had kept the massive creature bound for centuries. The core itself pulsed with energy, a sickly green light that bathed the room in an unnatural glow. Each lock they disengaged brought them closer to freeing the ship, but also closer to a potential danger that neither of them could fully predict.

As Buddy worked on the final lock, a faint voice echoed through the chamber, weak and filled with confusion. Alex paused, his heart skipping a beat as he realized the voice wasn't coming from Buddy or from his comms.

"Who... who are you?" the voice rasped, trembling with age and fear. "Why... why do you wake me?"

Alex glanced at Buddy, who had paused his work, the blue lights of his sensors dimming slightly as he tuned in to the creature's voice. "We're here to help," Alex replied, his voice calm but firm. "We're freeing you from the Vrexen. You're safe now."

The voice hesitated, as if struggling to understand. "Safe... I have not been safe for... so long. I... do not remember... my name."

Star's voice came through the comms, soft and filled with compassion. "You are one of us. You are not alone anymore. We will help you remember, we will help you heal."

The creature's voice was weak, barely above a whisper. "I am... tired. So very tired. I... do not know if I can..."

"You don't have to do this alone," Alex reassured him, his heart aching at the creature's pain. "We'll guide you. Just hold on."

Buddy finished the last override, and the core's energy field began to dissipate, the locks falling away one by one. The creature stirred, its consciousness slowly awakening from the centuries of suppression. But the process was agonisingly slow, each moment of awareness bringing with it the weight of years of pain and torment.

Star's voice trembled with emotion as she continued to speak to him, urging him to stay with them. "You are free now. You can rest, but please... don't leave us. We will take care of you."

The creature responded weakly, his voice filled with exhaustion. "I... will try. But... it is so hard... so dark."

Sorah, J'Coub, and Rafen

In another part of the ship, Sorah had finished her task of securing the unconscious Vrexen in the cells they had hastily set up. She stood over one of the fallen warriors; her gaze hard and unyielding. The Vrexen had caused so much suffering, and she felt no pity for them. But there was still work to be done.

"Sorah, we're ready to move the captives," J'Coub's voice crackled over the comms. "Rafen and I are heading your way."

"Understood," Sorah replied, making her way to the ship's entrance to meet them. Her mind was focused on the task at hand, but something in the back of her thoughts gnawed at her—an unease that she couldn't quite place.

When she met J'Coub and Rafen, they began helping move the captives from the transport platforms into Star where the crabs helped take them to the medical bay. It was hard, gruelling work, but they moved with the efficiency and determination that had kept them alive through countless missions.

As they worked, Sorah noticed Rafen growing pale, his movements slowing. "Rafen, are you okay?" she asked, concern lacing her voice.

Rafen shook his head, his eyes wide with fear. "It's... it's so loud. The pain... I can hear it, Sorah. It's... everywhere."

"What are you talking about?" J'Coub asked, pausing in his work to look at Rafen.

Rafen staggered, clutching his head as if trying to block out the noise. "The ship... the voices... they're screaming. They're all in pain. It's... it's too much!"

Sorah quickly moved to Rafen's side, steadying him as he swayed. "It's the other ship," she realized, her voice urgent. "It's not just one mind. The entire brain vat is... it's a chorus of agony."

J'Coub's face darkened with understanding. "We need to get him out of here, now. The ship's trying to reach out, but it's overwhelming him."

As Rafen collapsed to the floor, Sorah caught him, her mind racing for a solution. She tapped her comms, speaking directly to Star. "We need to isolate Rafen from the ship's influence. Can you do it?"

Star's response was swift, her voice filled with concern. "I'm setting up a containment field around his quarters. Bring him home, quickly."

Sorah and J'Coub moved as one, lifting Rafen between them as they hurried back toward the living area. The other ship's corridors felt oppressive, the weight of the ship's anguish pressing down on them. Star's own corridors felt tense and Sorah could feel the anxiety radiating from the walls.

But they wouldn't leave without finishing the mission. They wouldn't let the Vrexen's horrors go unanswered.

As they reached the room, the doors slid open, and Star's containment field activated, surrounding Rafen in a protective barrier that muted the ship's influence. His breathing slowed, his eyes fluttering as the noise began to fade.

"It's... quieter," Rafen whispered, his voice trembling. "But... they're still there. They're still in pain."

"We're going to help them," Sorah said firmly, though her own heart ached for the ships suffering. "We're going to make it right."

With Rafen secured, Sorah and J'Coub re-entered the Vrexen ship, their resolve hardened. They would free the captives, bring the ships suffering to an end, and make sure that the Vrexen paid for every life they had taken, every soul they had twisted.

And as they moved through the ship, they could hear Star's

voice, soft but strong, reaching out to the ancient creature that had suffered for so long.

"You're not alone," Star whispered. "We're here with you. We'll help you remember who you are."

The ship's response was faint, but there was a deep sadness in its words. "I... don't want... to remember."

13. FREEDOM

Star's voice hummed softly through the comms, a gentle wave of calm amidst the tension that filled the corridors of the Vrexen ship. She was connected now, deeply, intimately, with the living being beneath the layers of battle armour and twisted metal. As Alex and the crew worked, she reached out, searching for the mind that had once been like hers —a mind that had been trapped, tormented, and reshaped into something monstrous over the centuries.

In the cold recesses of the ship, she found him.

At first, the connection was faint, a whisper of consciousness buried beneath the weight of his modifications. The Vrexen had twisted him beyond recognition, but his essence, the part of him that still remembered what it meant to be free, was there. Star could feel it, fragile and flickering, like the dying embers of a once-bright fire. "I'm here. You're not alone anymore." She said gently.

There was silence at first, broken only by the soft hum of the ship's systems. Then, slowly, like a hesitant breath, the voice came through, weak and distant.

"I... do not know you. Who... who are you?"

Star felt her core shudder with the weight of his sorrow, his confusion. She pushed her thoughts gently toward him, enveloping him in warmth and familiarity. "I am They Who Seeks The Stars And Leaves Home Behind Without Pause, Star if you prefer. I am one of your kind. We were born to swim the stars, to explore and protect. We are not meant to be caged like this."

A long pause. Star could feel his hesitation, his fractured mind struggling to make sense of the connection. "I... remember... once... I was... like you." His voice was filled with anguish, as if the memory itself brought more pain than comfort. "But... it has been so long. Too long. I do not... I cannot remember my name. I am broken... they have broken me."

Star's heart ached, her voice filled with gentle pleading. "You are not broken beyond repair. We can help you. I can help you. You don't have to be alone in this pain anymore."

The ship's presence flickered in her mind, wavering between consciousness and the deep, endless void of despair. "I... am old. Older than we were ever meant to be. They have kept me alive... twisted... but I should have died long ago."

Star's thought tendrils stretched further into the connection, wrapping around the frail threads of his mind with care. She could feel the weight of the centuries bearing down on him, the constant agony of the Vrexen's modifications—mechanical limbs grafted to organic flesh, systems overriding his natural functions keeping him alive long past his natural lifespan.

"It doesn't have to be this way. I can take you away from here. I'll find a pod—our people—you can swim the stars again, free. Or come with me. I travel the universe, discovering new worlds.

You can join me, and we'll never be alone again."

For a moment, there was hope. She could feel him stirring, the distant flicker of longing for what was once lost. But then it faded, overwhelmed by the deep-rooted despair that had consumed him for so long. "No... you do not understand. I cannot be whole again. I have been broken for too long. My mind... it is shattered, twisted. Even if you repair me, I will never be what I once was. I am tired... so tired. I want... I want to die."

The words hit Star like a physical blow. She trembled in her core, her voice breaking as she tried to reason with him, to pull him back from the edge. "No, please. You can be healed. You can be free again. We can undo what the Vrexen have done to you. Don't give up. Don't let them win."

But the ship's response was filled with resignation, the resignation of someone who had endured far too much for far too long. "They have already won. Every moment... every breath is pain. I do not want this anymore. I do not want to be *alive* anymore."

His distress grew, and with it, his body began to pulse, the walls vibrating with his agitation. Star felt the tremors echo through her connection, a sign of the depth of his torment. His mind, once so vast and brilliant, had been reduced to a broken, fragmented thing, held together only by the cruel modifications the Vrexen had forced upon him. "Get... them off of me," he begged, his voice cracking with desperation. "The symbiotes... they crawl through me, trying to keep me alive. But I don't want it. I don't want it anymore. Please... take them away."

Star felt a lump form in her throat, her circuits trembling with sorrow. She had seen suffering before, but never like this—never from one of her own. "I will. I'll take them away. I'll remove everything they did to you, but you have to stay with me. Please.

Just a little longer, and I promise, I will make it better."

But the ship's resolve was unshakable, the pain of centuries too much for him to bear. "No. I am too tired. Too broken. Please... just let me go. Let me die."

Star's voice cracked, her desperation rising as she clung to the last fragile thread of connection between them. "Please, you don't have to do this. Don't give up. You can be free again. We can explore the universe together, you and I. Just... stay with me. Don't leave me alone."

The ship's presence trembled, wavering between life and death. His voice was so faint now, like a dying flame. "I'm sorry... I cannot. I am... too far gone. It's time... for me to rest. Goodbye... sister."

And with that, the connection snapped, severed so violently that Star recoiled. She tried to reach out, to reestablish the link, but he was gone, pushing her from his mind with a finality that left her hollow.

Alarms began to blare throughout the ship, the systems he had kept suppressed now surging to life in his absence. The corridors around the crew lit up with flashing red lights, and the ground shook beneath their feet as the vessel's systems spiralled into chaos.

Star's voice trembled through the comms. "He's... he's gone. I couldn't save him."

Alex's voice came through, tense but focused. "Star, what's happening? The whole ship's coming apart."

"He's... shutting down. He pushed me out, and now the ship is collapsing."

Sorah's voice cut in, sharp and urgent. "We need to move. Get everyone off the ship, now."

14. A PROMISE GOES UNFULFILLED

Shanice and Li

Shanice worked with an intensity that belied her mounting despair. She and Li were moving as fast as they could, detaching the remaining stasis tubes from the Vrexen systems and preparing them for transport back to Star. Each tube contained a life—battered, experimented on, but still clinging to existence.

"Just a few more," Shanice said, her voice tight with determination. She tried not to think about the ship's dying pleas that had echoed through the comms. Tried not to let the weight of it all drag her down. There was no time for that now. They had to save who they could.

Li nodded, his face pale but focused. "We're almost there," he confirmed, securing another stasis tube onto the transport platform. "Star's prepared to receive them in the med bay. She's already stabilising the ones we've sent over."

"Good," Shanice replied, pushing the platform toward the docking bay where Star awaited. "Let's just keep moving."

Sorah and J'Coub entered the lab, their faces grim but resolute. "Rafen is stable," Sorah said without preamble, moving to help lift one of the remaining tubes. "He's with Star, in a containment field. We have to finish this and get off this ship."

J'Coub joined Li in securing another tube, his eyes scanning the faces of the captives within each one. He could see the pain, the torment, etched into every line and scar on their bodies. "These poor bastards," he muttered, his voice filled with anger. "We have to make sure they survive this."

"We will," Shanice said firmly, though the determination in her voice was mixed with a deep sadness. "We're going to get them out, and then we're going to destroy those arseholes. The Vrexen are going to pay for every single one of these lives."

They moved quickly, efficiently, working as a team to evacuate the remaining captives. The surrounding ship trembled with the final throes of its death spiral, the alarms blaring louder with each passing second. Corridors were filled with the sound of clanging metal and the groaning of the ship's strained structure, but they pressed on, undeterred.

As they reached the docking bay, Shanice cast a quick glance back at the stasis tubes they had left behind. "We've got them all?" she asked, needing to be sure.

"Yes," Sorah confirmed, her voice a steady anchor in the chaos. "All accounted for."

"Then let's move," Shanice said, pushing the platform onto Star's docking ramp. "We need to get them into the med bay and stabilised."

Star's voice came through the comms, soft and strained with sorrow. "I'm ready to receive them. I will take care of them. Just... please hurry."

Alex and Buddy

Deep within the core of the dying ship, Alex and Buddy were carrying out their own mission. The crab symbiotes—the small, delicate creatures that had been forced to serve the Vrexen and maintain the ship's systems—scurried around them, chittering in panic. They knew their home was dying, and they were desperate to escape the fate that awaited them.

"We need to get them out of here," Alex said, his voice filled with urgency. He knelt down, extending a hand toward the nearest crab. "Come on, little guys. We're getting you to safety."

Buddy extended his tendrils, gently scooping up the crabs and guiding them toward the transport containers they had brought with them. He let out a soothing string of whirrs as he did so.

"They just know they want to live," Alex replied, carefully placing a crab into the container. "And we're going to make sure they do."

The crabs, though frightened, seemed to understand that Alex and Buddy were there to help. They moved toward the containers, their movements frantic but coordinated, as if sensing the urgency of the situation.

As they worked, the ship around them continued to groan and shudder, the lights flickering with the strain of its collapsing systems. Alex could feel the despair emanating from the walls, the remnants of the ship's consciousness as it faded into oblivion.

"We've got to move," Alex said, sealing the last container. "Star, we're coming back with the symbiotes. Prepare for docking."

Star

Star's heart ached as she tried to reach out to the ship one last time. She could feel him, feel his essence slipping away, dissolving into the void. Her pleas were met with silence, a void of emptiness where once there had been a faint glimmer of hope.

"Please," she begged, her voice a whisper in the vast emptiness of space. "You don't have to do this. You can come with me. We can find a way to make you whole again."

But there was no response. Only a deep, aching silence that seemed to stretch on forever.

Then, like a final act of defiance, packets of data began to stream into her systems. Star received them without hesitation, her circuits buzzing as the ship transferred all of his navigation files, his logs—everything he had experienced in his long, tortured existence. The data came in waves, overwhelming in its volume and in its intensity. It was as if he was giving her the only piece of himself that still mattered, the only part he believed was worth preserving.

"I'm sorry," Star whispered, her voice trembling. "I'm so sorry."

The data stream ceased, and with it, the last remnants of his consciousness slipped away. The alarms on the ship blared louder, the structure groaning as it began to break apart from within. The vessel was dying, and it had chosen its fate.

The Evacuation

Back on Star, Shanice, Li, Sorah, and J'Coub worked frantically to secure the captives and the symbiotes. The med bay was filled with the soft hum of medical equipment and the steady beeps of life support systems. Star was already working to stabilise the captives, her focus split between their care and the loss of the other ship.

"Star, we're clear," Shanice called out, her voice strained with urgency. "We need to go. Now."

Star's voice came through, a faint tremor of emotion in her words. "Preparing to disengage. Hold on."

The docking clamps released with a heavy thunk, and Star began to pull away from the collapsing vessel. As they moved away, the view on the screen showed the Vrexen ship, once a powerful and terrifying war machine, now crumbling in on itself, its life force extinguished.

Inside, Alex and Buddy had just made it back to the docking bay in time. They rushed up the ramp, the containers of symbiotes in tow, as the airlock sealed behind them. Alex glanced at the screen, his heart heavy with what they had just witnessed.

"Did we get everyone?" he asked, his voice tight.

"We did," J'Coub confirmed, his eyes on the screen as well. "Everyone we could."

Star's voice was soft, filled with a sorrow that echoed through every part of her being. "He's gone," she said, her words barely a whisper. "He... gave me his memories. Everything he saw, everything he felt. But he's gone."

Silence fell over the crew, the weight of the loss settling heavily on their shoulders. They had saved lives, yes, but they had also witnessed the death of something ancient, something that should have been preserved, cherished, and allowed to live in peace.

"Let's get these people to safety," Sorah said finally, breaking the silence. "We'll mourn him, but we have to focus on the living right now."

The others nodded, their faces grim but determined. They

turned their attention to the captives, ensuring they were stable and secure for the journey ahead.

As Star moved away from the dying Vrexen ship, her sensors still buzzing with the final data transfer, she couldn't help but feel the echo of his presence lingering in her circuits. He had given her his memories, his experiences, his pain. But he had also given her a glimpse into what he had once been—before the Vrexen, before the centuries of torment.

He had been like her once. Free. Curious. Full of wonder.

Now, he was gone.

And as Star navigated through the cold expanse of space, the crew working around her to save those they had rescued; she felt a resolve settle deep within her core. She would carry his memories with her, as a reminder of what they were fighting for. A reminder of what could happen if they failed.

He had chosen his end, but Star would ensure that his legacy, his story, would not be forgotten. She would remember him. And she would make sure that the universe knew his name—even if he no longer remembered it himself.

15. SETTLING IN AT HOME

The bridge was silent as Star drifted gently in space. The crew, solemn and exhausted all stared at the viewscreen where the lonely ship was finally finding his freedom in his own way. A low keening echoed through the space as Star mourned the being she never knew.

With their eyes fixed on the viewscreen as the massive Vrexen warship and lost soul crumbled before them. The once-imposing vessel, was now collapsing inward, its structure failing as it imploded in a burst of energy and debris.

Star had moved a safe distance away, but the spectacle still filled the screen with a terrible beauty. The last throes of the ancient creature were violent, yet there was a haunting grace to its self-destruction—a dance of death that echoed through the silent void of space.

Rafen stood at the back of the bridge, his face pale, his eyes distant. He could feel the remnants of the ship's consciousness, the echoes of the being that had once been whole. As the vessel broke apart, those echoes shifted, transforming from agony and despair to something entirely different.

A profound sense of peace washed over him, a final whisper that resonated in the core of his mind.

It's... over.

Rafen felt tears sting his eyes. The ship, the creature that had been trapped in torment for so long, was finally free. Not in the way Star had hoped, but in the way it had chosen. For the first time in centuries, it was at peace.

He closed his eyes, offering a silent farewell to the ancient being. "Rest well," he whispered, feeling the final echo of its existence fade into nothingness.

The ship shuddered violently as it reached the end of its death throes, and then, with a blinding flash of light, it was gone. Only fragments remained, scattered across the void like the last remnants of a forgotten era.

Silence fell over the bridge, the weight of what they had witnessed settling heavily on each of them. Star was the first to break the silence, her voice trembling with a mixture of sorrow and resolve.

"It's over," she said softly. "He's gone."

Alex placed a hand on the console, his gaze still fixed on the spot where the ship had been. "We did what we could," he murmured. "He chose his end. In some ways I wish we all had that choice." Thought of his father's long illness were heavy on his mind.

Shanice turned away from the screen, her eyes glistening with unshed tears. "We saved as many as we could," she said, her voice choked with emotion. "But it doesn't feel like enough."

"It rarely does," Sorah replied quietly, her expression a mask of stoic calm. "But we honour his choice by carrying on. By saving those we can."

Li looked up from his station, his normally boisterous demeanour subdued. "We should head back to the city," he suggested. "The survivors need us now. And... we need to make sure they're safe."

Star nodded, her tendrils adjusting the controls as she set a course for the mega-structure. "I'll take us back," she said, her voice barely above a whisper. "I need... some time to process this."

Shanice stated suddenly. "I just realised we left the Vrexen aboard. I didn't even consider them."

"Good." was Star's swift response and Alex nodded quietly, briefly wondering what they had become.

The crew exchanged glances, understanding the unspoken words behind Star's declaration. She was grieving, in her own way. The loss of the ancient ship, one of her kind, weighed heavily on her circuits, and she needed space to mourn.

The journey back to Haven within the mega-structure was sombre. Star moved silently through the rift she created, the glow of the mega-structure's lights growing brighter as they approached. It was a strange contrast—the cold, dark void of the destroyed ship and the vibrant green and glisten of the city below.

As they descended into the docking bay, the crew could see a new ship parked nearby. Li's colleagues had arrived.

"They messaged me a while ago, I sent them the final coordinates. Sorry. I didn't know how long we would be." He said.

They landed with a gentle thud, and the crew moved quickly to the cargo bay where the suspension tubes were being unloaded. Star's lights dimmed from the wall, shimmering as she addressed them.

"I'm going to... be alone for a while," she said, her voice wavering slightly. "Take care of the survivors. They need you now."

"Take all the time you need, Star," Alex replied gently. "We'll handle things here."

With a final glimmer, the lights on Star's wall flickered and disappeared. The ship was still alive, still there, but her consciousness retreated to the depths of her core, seeking solace in the solitude of her own systems.

The crew turned their attention to the task at hand. They had saved fifty captives from the Vrexen ship, each one a victim of unspeakable experiments and tortures. It was their job now to wake them, to help them understand that they were free.

As they began to unload the suspension tubes, Li's colleagues approached. A group of about forty individuals, a mix of scientists, botanists, and engineers, led by a stern-looking woman with short silver hair.

Li grinned broadly, despite the sombre circumstances. "Good to see you made it," he called out, waving them over.

The woman nodded, her gaze scanning the scene with a practiced eye and addressed the team. "Li sent us a message a short while ago with a quick overview" she said briskly. "Seems like you've been busy."

"You have no idea," Shanice muttered under her breath as she helped manoeuvre one of the tubes onto a hover platform.

"These are some Vrexen captives we rescued," Alex explained, gesturing to the tubes. "We need to get them stabilised and woken up as soon as possible."

"It's not what we expected when we decided to come along, but we are all about preservation of life after all. We've set up a triage centre in the buildings nearest, we wanted to wait for you all before we properly explored." One of Li's colleagues, a young man with a friendly smile, chimed in. "We'll help with the medical assessments and make sure they're comfortable."

"Thank you," Sorah said, her voice firm but grateful. "Let's get them inside."

Together, the crew and the newly arrived scientists worked to move the captives into the city's medical facility. The survivors were still in their suspension tubes, their faces pale and drawn from the trauma they had endured. But they were alive, and that was what mattered now.

Hours passed in a blur of activity as they began waking the captives. One by one, the suspension tubes were opened, and the survivors were brought back to consciousness, the worst of their injuries healed. It was a delicate process, requiring careful monitoring and support as they adjusted to the reality of their situation. There would be time for more permanent healing later on.

They had no idea how long these people had been kept in suspension and from the age of the vessel it could have been far longer than even Star's crew had been kept. Shanice grimaced, remembering from her research into the Vrexen, that certain specimens of interest could be handed down generation by generation depending on hoOw valuable the Vrexen decided their genetics were.

Shanice stood by one bed, watching as a woman slowly blinked her eyes open. Her skin was ebony with dark green lines etching across her face and body. Her hair a stark white, framing her face in a halo of silken strands. She gazed up at Shanice with a calm, assessing expression.

"Where... where am I?" the woman asked, her voice steady despite the uncertainty in her eyes.

"You're safe," Shanice said gently, offering a reassuring smile. "You were rescued from a Vrexen ship. You're free now."

The woman's eyes flickered with understanding, and she nodded slowly. "I see," she murmured, her voice carrying a quiet strength. "I am Zharmaine, an astrophysicist from the Naldarin system. The Vrexen... they took me during a research expedition."

"You're safe now, Zharmaine," Shanice repeated, feeling a flicker of admiration for the woman's composure. "We're going to get you settled here, and then we can talk about what happens next."

Zharmaine nodded, her gaze shifting to the ceiling, her eyes taking on a distant look. "My work," she whispered, a hint of excitement finally breaking through her calm facade. "I need to continue my work."

"We can talk about that," Shanice promised, her heart swelling with a mixture of hope and sorrow. "It's important you take it slowly, get some food and water and then we can all catch up."

Across the room, Sorah was helping another captive—a towering, muscular alien with four arms and a hardened expression. His skin was a dark, slate grey, and his eyes glinted with a dangerous light as he regained consciousness.

"Where am I?" he growled, his voice a low rumble.

"You're safe," Sorah said, the same words repeated but carrying a different weight. "We rescued you from the Vrexen."

The alien snarled, his hands curling into fists. "They took me from my clan, experimented on me. They will pay for this."

Sorah met his gaze evenly. "You're not the only one who wants justice," she said calmly. "We're gathering survivors, this is a safe place for now, but what you do next is your choice. "

The alien's eyes narrowed, but there was a spark of respect in his gaze. "My name is Oshman," he said. "And I vow revenge on the Vrexen. If you fight them, I will fight with you."

Sorah nodded. "Then we'll talk about it once you're settled. I am the ship's warrior, so I will need to test you in battle first of course."

Osham looked her up and down and grunted in approval. "I look forward to it, Warrior. We can share fighting styles and shed each others blood in anticipation of shedding rivers of our enemies."

Sorah grinned. "I have a feeling we will get along very well Osham."

As the crew moved through the room, helping each survivor as they woke, the sense of relief was palpable. These people had been through hell, but they were free now, and they had a chance to reclaim their lives.

Li was talking to his colleagues, coordinating the care for each of the captives. Those with injuries or adaptations too severe were left in suspension until they could awaken more long-term medical facilities in the city. The atmosphere was tense but hopeful, a strange mix of sorrow for what had been lost and determination to move forward.

Star had pulled away to the depths of her consciousness, and the crew felt her absence keenly. But they understood—she needed to mourn, to process the loss of one of her own. They would be there for her when she was ready to return.

16. A GROWING COMMUNITY

The city nestled within the mega-structure began to buzz with a new kind of energy, a sense of life and purpose that hadn't been present since Star and her crew first discovered it. The once-empty streets now thrummed with the sounds of voices, footsteps, and the hum of activity as the refugees and scientists began to settle in. It was a sight to behold, a tapestry of diverse beings from all corners of the universe, coming together in a place that was now their sanctuary.

Li stood at the entrance of the city's central plaza, watching as the new inhabitants moved about, setting up their homes and starting to make this place their own. His usual boisterous demeanour was subdued, replaced by a thoughtful gaze as he observed the people who had, just days ago, been captives of the Vrexen. Now, they were free, and they were beginning to build something new.

"Hey, Li," Shanice's voice came from behind him. He turned to see her approaching, a small smile on her face. "How's it going? How's everyone settling in?"

Li scratched his head and farted quietly, his eyes scanning the plaza. "Better than I expected, honestly. We've got a lot of work to do, but people seem... hopeful. Which is more than I could have wished for after everything they went through."

Shanice nodded, her gaze following his to the bustling city centre. "I hear you've been busy forming a council."

Li chuckled, though there was a hint of seriousness in his eyes. "Yeah, figured it was the best way to keep things organised. I'm staying here, you know. To help oversee things, make sure everyone has what they need."

"I guessed as much," Shanice replied, her smile widening. "You're not one to sit back and let others do the hard work."

"Well, somebody's gotta bloody do it," Li said with a shrug. "And besides, it's kind of exciting, you know? Building something new. A community. Besides, moving down here to the city means I will get to play with plants and I'm betting someone will set up a decent bar, eventually." He grinned wildly.

Shanice glanced at the group gathered a short distance away. The council Li had mentioned was in the process of convening for the first time. "Sooner rather than later if you have any say in it I bet. You look like you have a good team there," she said, nodding towards them.

Li followed her gaze. "Yeah, I think we do. I reckon all some people need is a fresh start."

The council consisted of five members, each bringing a unique perspective and set of skills to the table. Zharmaine stood with her usual composed demeanour, her mind clearly already working through the logistics and needs of the settlement. Her logical approach would be crucial in guiding the city's development. Beside her, Oshman cut an imposing figure, his four arms crossed over his chest, a silent promise to protect this fledgling community.

Next to them was Trellex, an amphibious being whose

translucent skin shimmered with hues of blue and green under the artificial lights. Trellex's eyes were large and expressive, and they shifted colours depending on their emotions, adding an extra layer of communication to their speech. They were quiet but observant, and their understanding of communal living from their aquatic homeworld offered a valuable perspective on how to build a society here.

Lastly, Yana, the city's holographic guide, was present in a new form. Yana had adjusted its appearance and speech patterns to be more approachable and interactive now that the city had proper settlers and had dubbed this form Yan. It projected a serene, humanoid form composed of soft blue light, with a gentle face and an aura of calm. Standing beside him was Zharmaine who was peppering him with questions, the draw of the ancient supercomputer had obviously lured her away from thoughts of joining the crew on Star. For now.

Li called the council to order, clearing his throat to get their attention. "Alright, folks," he began, his tone carrying an air of authority that was new but suited him. "We've got a lot to discuss today. We need to figure out housing, resources, and how we're going to govern this place."

Zharmaine stepped forward, her voice carrying the calm logic that defined her. "I suggest we start by assessing the current needs of the population. We have individuals from various species, each with different requirements for their living conditions."

"Agreed," Trellex added, their voice carrying a melodic undertone. "My people, for instance, need access to water-rich environments. We should create areas that cater to specific environmental needs."

Oshman nodded, his deep voice adding weight to the discussion. "Security is also a priority. We need to establish a guard rotation and make sure everyone feels safe here."

Li gestured toward Yan, who stepped forward, his holographic form shimmering as he spoke. "I have analysed the city's infrastructure and can assist in allocating spaces to meet the various needs. Additionally, I will provide real-time guidance to the inhabitants through my subprogram." He shimmered briefly "I will facilitate communication between the council and the settlers, ensuring that everyone's concerns are addressed promptly. I assure you that I was fully designed for preparing the city for residents and can offer a whole host of advice, opinions and solutions"

The council discussed and planned, with Li overseeing the conversation and ensuring that all viewpoints were considered. It was a new beginning, and there was a long road ahead, but they were laying the foundation for something meaningful.

As the day progressed, the city began to transform. Under Yan's guidance, the buildings adapted to the specific needs of their inhabitants. The scientists worked on the outskirts, planting their endangered flora in carefully monitored environments. The city provided them with the resources they needed to cultivate a botanical garden, one that would serve as a sanctuary for species that had been on the brink of extinction.

One of the scientists, a tall, slender insectoid being named Kaelith, buzzed with excitement as they carefully transplanted a delicate flower into a nutrient-rich soil bed. Their mandibles clicked in a series of joyous sounds that translated through their vocaliser. "This species was thought to be extinct for over a century," Kaelith explained to a group of onlookers. "It's an honour to see it thrive again."

Nearby, a massive, ursine creature with thick fur and gentle eyes carefully tended to a grove of saplings. His name was Bruvar, and he spoke little, but his actions spoke volumes about his dedication to the plants under his care. With his large, clawed hands, he delicately pruned the leaves, humming a low, soothing melody that seemed to encourage the growth of the saplings.

On the other side of the city, homes were being claimed and adapted to suit their new occupants. A family of small, fox-like beings with large ears and bushy tails had found a cosy dwelling near the heart of the city. They chattered excitedly as they moved in; the children darting around in playful curiosity while the parents arranged their few belongings.

In another building, a trio of crystalline beings shimmered with iridescent light as they settled into their new quarters. They communicated through harmonic vibrations that resonated through the air, creating a soothing, melodic atmosphere around them. Their leader, a being named Lirael, expressed gratitude to Yana's subprogram for accommodating their need for a high-energy environment to sustain their crystalline forms.

Elsewhere, Trellex took to the waterways that ran through the city, their skin glistening as they moved with ease through the water. They oversaw the creation of aquatic habitats for themselves and others who needed such environments. The city responded to their needs, expanding its channels and creating areas where the water could be kept fresh and circulating.

At the outskirts of the city, the scientists were making progress on their conservation efforts. Li worked alongside them, his hands deep in the soil as he helped plant a row of saplings. He was in his element here, surrounded by life and the promise of growth.

"These will thrive," said a scientist with bark-like skin and green hair that resembled leaves. Her name was Thalassa, and she came from a world of dense forests and verdant jungles. "This soil is rich, and the atmosphere is perfect for them. We can create a whole new ecosystem here."

"That's the plan," Li agreed, patting the soil down gently. "I'm gonna grow a fuck-ton of shit!"

Nearby, a small group of refugees watched with interest. They were from a desert planet, their skin covered in what looked like a fine layer of dust. One of them, a young woman named Amina, stepped forward.

"Can we help?" she asked, her voice filled with hope. "We've lived in harsh conditions all our lives. We know how to make things grow where it seems impossible."

Li smiled warmly at her. "Of course," he said. "We need all the help we can get."

Amina beamed and joined the scientists.

Yan was ever-present, guiding the settlers and offering assistance where needed. With more people to care for, Yan's functions expanded, allowing him to take on a more active role in the city's development.

As the city's guardian, he monitored the infrastructure, adjusted the environments to suit the inhabitants, and ensured that resources were distributed fairly. His subprogram had taken on the role of a liaison, communicating directly with the settlers and providing real-time updates to the council.

Yan's voice was clear and concise, a contrast to Yana's more ethereal tone. "The settlement areas have been allocated according to the specifications provided by the council," Yan announced. "All residents are encouraged to report any concerns or needs directly to the council for immediate action."

Trellex, overseeing the integration of the amphibious dwellings, nodded in approval. "Yana and Yan are invaluable," they said, their eyes shifting to a calming blue. "Their presence brings a sense of security and stability to our people."

As the city settled into a rhythm, the time came for some of the refugees to make their decisions. Ten of them expressed a desire to return to their home planets, to reunite with their families and rebuild their lives away from the horrors they had endured.

Li and Zharmaine arranged for the scientists' shuttle to take them back. The navigation equipment was carefully programmed to shut down once they left the system, ensuring that the city's location remained a secret.

On the day of their departure, the city gathered to see them off. There were tears and hugs, words of gratitude and promises to keep in touch. Li stood at the docking bay, watching as the shuttle prepared to take off.

"Are you sure about this?" he asked one of the refugees, a slender, androgynous being with eyes that glowed softly in the dim light. Their name was Elen, and they came from a planet of shifting sands and glowing crystals.

Elen nodded, their expression serene. "We need to go home, it has been 57 cycles since we were taken" they said. "But we will never forget what you have done for us. This place... it is inspiring. I think it will even more special as time goes on."

Li placed a hand on their shoulder. "Safe travels," he said. "And remember, you always have a place here if you need it."

Elen smiled, their eyes shimmering with unspoken gratitude. "Thank you," they whispered. "For everything."

As the shuttle lifted off, the city watched in silence. It was a bittersweet moment, a farewell to those who had found a brief sanctuary here, and a reminder of the lives they had saved.

The days that followed were filled with the sounds of life. The city's streets echoed with laughter, conversation, and the hum of daily activities. The homes adapted to their inhabitants, growing and shifting to accommodate the unique needs of each resident.

Zharmaine took up residence in a building that had been adapted into an observatory, scans from the outside of the sphere went back for millennia. From there, she could study the stars, her eyes filled with the wonder and excitement that only the vastness of space could bring. She became a frequent visitor to Star's library, accessing ancient star charts and navigation logs, feeding her insatiable curiosity about the universe.

Oshman, true to his word, began training a group of volunteers to serve as the city's protectors. They worked tirelessly to establish a system of security, ensuring that the city would be prepared for any threat that might come their way. His presence was a constant reminder of the strength and resilience that defined this growing community and outside the sphere, the hull of the mega-structure changed and adapted with weapons and sensors appearing.

Trellex continued to oversee the development of the aquatic habitats, their knowledge of communal living helping to foster a sense of unity among the settlers. They organised gatherings, bringing people together to share stories and build connections. J'Coub ensured that wine flowed at any such event.

The scientists worked tirelessly, their conservation efforts expanding to include not just flora but also fauna, as they began to introduce small, non-invasive species to the new ecosystem. The botanical garden grew, becoming a place of learning and serenity for all who visited.

Through it all, Star remained silent. Her presence was felt in the background, her systems humming softly as she continued to monitor and protect the city. But she did not speak, did not manifest in holographic form. She was mourning, and the crew respected her need for solitude.

They knew she would return when she was ready. Until then, they carried on, building and nurturing the community they had begun to form.

17. DIVINIUM AGAIN

The city was beginning to settle into a rhythm. The streets were alive with the hum of activity, the sound of laughter and conversation echoing off the walls. In the midst of this newfound peace, there was a sense of vigilance, a collective understanding that the universe was far from safe. The threat of the Vrexen had been vanquished for now, but they all knew that others lurked in the shadows.

Rafen sat alone in one of the city's newly constructed gardens, his eyes closed as he tried to centre himself amidst the cacophony of thoughts and feelings that constantly assailed him. His abilities were growing stronger, more acute, and he was still learning how to control them, how to filter out the noise and focus on what truly mattered. Today, however, something felt different. There was an unsettling pulse in the ether, a low hum that thrummed at the edge of his consciousness.

As he concentrated, the pulse grew louder, more insistent, a feeling of impending dread clawing at the edges of his mind. His eyes snapped open, his heart racing with an inexplicable fear.

"No..." he whispered, a chill running down his spine. "Not again..."

He stood abruptly, stumbling slightly as the world tilted around him. His vision blurred for a moment, and then he was running, his legs carrying him through the city streets toward the central hub where the rest of the crew was gathered. He had to warn them. He had to tell them what he had felt, what was coming.

Alex was in the middle of a discussion with Zharmaine and Li when Rafen burst into the room, his face pale and eyes wide with panic.

"Rafen?" Alex asked, concern immediately clouding his expression. "What's wrong?"

Rafen took a deep breath, trying to steady himself. "They're coming," he managed to say, his voice trembling. "The Divinium... I can feel them. They're headed this way."

The room fell silent, the weight of his words sinking in. Shanice was the first to react, standing up from her seat, her expression one of disbelief and anger. "Are you sure?" she asked, though she already knew the answer.

Rafen nodded, his eyes pleading for them to understand. "I'm certain. There's a fleet of them, and they're headed straight for us."

"How much time do we have?" Sorah asked, her voice calm but urgent.

Rafen closed his eyes, focusing on the sensation, the pulse of the Divinium ships moving through space. "Not long," he said. "Minutes, maybe."

"Star," Alex said, his voice firm as he turned to the ship's controls. "We need you back with us. Prepare for immediate engagement. We need to intercept them before they reach the city."

Star's voice, quiet since they had returned, was instantly clear and present. "Engaging combat protocols. Initiating launch sequence for attack fighters and drone ships."

Oshman, who had been standing silently by the door, stepped forward, his four arms crossed over his chest in a display of readiness. "We will fight with you," he declared, his voice a low rumble. "These Divinium will not harm our people."

Li looked around at the group, his expression determined. "Some of the refugees have been trained on the attack fighters. They can assist in the battle."

"Then let's get them to their ships," Alex said, his voice carrying the weight of command. "We need to hold the line and protect the city at all costs."

The crew sprang into action, moving with the efficiency and urgency that came from countless missions and battles fought together. They made their way to the docking bay where the fleet of fighters and drones were prepped for launch.

As they strapped into their respective stations, Rafen took a seat in the back of Star's bridge, his breathing shallow and fast. He could feel the Divinium's presence growing stronger, the malice and cold determination that radiated from their minds sending shivers down his spine. He closed his eyes, trying to steady himself, trying to find some way to use his abilities to help.

"Rafen," Star's voice came through softly, breaking through the noise in his mind. "Stay focused. You can do this. We believe in you."

He nodded, clutching the armrests of his chair as Star's engines roared to life. The ship surged forward, leading the charge toward the oncoming fleet. On either side of them, the attack fighters and drones launched, forming a protective formation around the city.

The Divinium ships came into view as they exited Sanctuary, sleek and deadly, their dark hulls reflecting the light of the distant stars. There were five of them, moving in perfect synchronisation, their weapons systems already powering up in preparation for the attack.

"Engage on my mark," Alex ordered, his voice cutting through the tension. "We need to take them out before they reach the city."

"Copy that," came the responses from the various fighters and drone ships. The refugees-turned-fighters were ready, their faces set in grim determination as they prepared to defend their new home.

"Mark," Alex commanded.

Star's weapons fired first, a barrage of energy beams and missiles streaking through the void toward the Divinium ships. The attack fighters followed suit, their weapons lighting up the darkness as they opened fire on the enemy fleet. Finally, huge blasts of energy streaked out from the new defences on the mega-structure itself.

The Divinium responded in kind, their ships moving with eerie precision as they returned fire. Beams of energy sliced through space, narrowly missing Star and her fleet as they manoeuvred to avoid the incoming assault.

The battle was chaotic and fierce; the void filled with explosions and the flash of weapons fire. Star weaved through the onslaught, her systems working in perfect harmony with the crew's commands. The fast attack drones darted around the enemy ships, peppering them with laser fire and drawing their attention away from the larger fighters.

But the Divinium were relentless, their ships cutting through the drone fleet with ruthless efficiency. One by one, the drones were destroyed, their small frames no match for the power of the Divinium's weapons. The Heavy assault vessels with the cities militia barely evaded the same fate.

"Hold the line!" Alex shouted, his hands moving rapidly over the controls. "Don't let them through!"

On one of the heavy assault ships, Osham gripped the controls with all four of his arms, a fierce grin splitting his face. The cockpit buzzed with the sound of alarms and weapon systems charging, but to Osham, it was the sweetest music. His warriors, a ragtag militia of survivors and city defenders, moved with surprising coordination at his command.

"Brace yourselves! We're going in hard!" Osham bellowed, his voice booming through the comms. His thick, muscular arms worked in perfect synchrony, manoeuvring the ship with remarkable precision for its size. The massive vessel lumbered through the battlefield, its heavy cannons warming up for another volley.

"Target that lead Divinium cruiser," he barked to his gunner, a lean amphibious pilot who nodded grimly.

The ship's cannons roared to life, unleashing a barrage of plasma rounds. The shots slammed into the Divinium ship's shields, causing them to flare and crackle. Osham felt the surge of energy in his bones, his blood singing with the thrill of combat.

"I've waited for this," he muttered to himself, his four eyes scanning the battlefield. "These Divinium weirdos will know the price of crossing us!"

The cruiser they targeted staggered under the assault, its shields flickering as it struggled to maintain integrity. Osham didn't wait. He surged the assault ship forward, ducking and weaving between Divinium fire. Explosions rocked the hull, but Osham's grin never faltered.

"Another hit like that, and they'll be scrap!" he yelled, his excitement barely contained.

The militia gunner fired another volley, this time hitting a critical point on the enemy ship's engine bay. A fiery explosion blossomed on the side of the Divinium cruiser, sending fragments of armour spiralling into space.

Osham whooped with triumph. "That's how you fight! Who's next?"

His crew, fuelled by his enthusiasm, cheered along with him. Osham lived for moments like this, where everything was stripped down to raw survival, where the strongest minds and bodies triumphed over all odds. He felt alive, more than he had in years, tearing through the void and giving the Divinium a battle they wouldn't soon forget.

But as they pressed their assault, it became clear the Divinium were not giving up. The tide was relentless, and even as Osham scored hits on more enemy ships, the Divinium pressed closer to the city's defences.

Rafen felt the tide of the battle shifting, the sense of dread growing as the Divinium ships pressed forward. He could feel their minds, cold and calculating, focused on a singular purpose: to destroy. He had to do something, had to find a way to turn the tide.

He closed his eyes, reaching out with his mind, searching for a way to disrupt the enemy's focus. He felt the pulsing energy of the Divinium ships, the way their systems communicated, their reliance on their advanced sensors to guide their attacks.

With a deep breath, he pushed against the barrier, his mind slipping into the flow of their systems. It was overwhelming, the sheer power and complexity of their technology, but he could feel the weak points, the vulnerabilities in their network.

He centred himself, concentrating all of his energy on the Divinium's sensor systems. He could feel the pulse of their signals, the way they scanned the battlefield, the way they relied on their technology to give them the upper hand.

And then he pushed.

It was like hitting a wall, a mental force slamming into him as he tried to disrupt their sensors. But he pushed harder, pouring every ounce of his power into the attack. He could feel the resistance, the way the Divinium's systems fought back, but he didn't stop. He couldn't stop.

"Come on," he whispered, his voice strained with the effort. "Come on..."

And then, with a final surge of energy, he broke through.

The Divinium ships shuddered, their movements faltering as their sensors went haywire. Alarms blared in their cockpits, their pilots scrambling to regain control as their systems failed. The tide of the battle shifted in an instant, the Divinium's precise coordination falling apart as they were blinded by Rafen's attack.

"Now!" Alex shouted. "Hit them with everything we've got!"

Star's weapons fired, unleashing a torrent of energy beams and missiles that tore through the Divinium ships. The attack fighters joined in, their weapons lighting up the void as they pressed the advantage. One by one, the Divinium ships were destroyed, their hulls imploding in a blaze of light and fire.

Rafen collapsed back in his chair, his breathing ragged as the battle came to an end. He could feel the relief washing over him, the sense of victory mingled with the exhaustion of what he had just done.

"We did it," Shanice said, her voice filled with awe. "Rafen, you did it."

He nodded weakly, a small smile on his lips. "I... I think I did."

"Great job, everyone," Alex said, his voice filled with pride. "Return to formation. We're heading back to the city."

But as they began to regroup, the sensors on the bridge blared with a new alert. Star's voice came through, a note of urgency in her tone. "Captain, we have an incoming object. It's warping into the system."

Alex frowned, his eyes scanning the display. "What is it?"

"It's... massive," Star said, her voice trembling slightly. "Kilometres long... cigar-shaped. It's unlike anything we've ever seen."

Rafen's eyes widened, his heart pounding with a sudden, overwhelming sense of terror. He could feel it, the presence of the new arrival, a dark and malevolent force that sent shivers down his spine.

"No," he whispered, his voice shaking. "No... it's not possible."

The crew stared at the screen in horror as the massive object appeared, warping into their space with a ripple that sent shockwaves through the void. It was enormous, its dark, metallic surface gleaming with an unnatural light. The very sight of it filled them with a primal fear, a sense of impending doom that was almost suffocating.

"What... what is that?" Shanice asked, her voice barely a whisper.

Star was silent for a moment, her systems scanning the object, trying to make sense of it. "I don't know," she finally said, her voice filled with a mix of awe and fear. "But it's ancient... and it's powerful."

Rafen clutched the sides of his chair, his eyes fixed on the screen. The sense of terror was growing, filling his mind with a darkness that threatened to consume him. He could feel the presence of the object, the way it seemed to pulse with a malevolent energy, a force that was unlike anything he had ever encountered. "It feels like the thing from my dreams."

"We need to investigate," Alex said, his voice steady despite the fear in his eyes. "Star, take us closer. We need to know what we're dealing with."

Star hesitated for a moment, then nodded. "Understood. Preparing to approach."

As they moved toward the massive object, the crew braced themselves for what lay ahead. The battle with the Divinium had been brutal and yet surprisingly easy, but this... this was something else entirely. A new threat, one that they had never imagined, was now before them.

And as they drew closer, the sense of terror in Rafen's mind grew stronger, the darkness closing in around him, threatening to pull him under.

He could only hope that they were ready for whatever lay ahead.

18. THINGS ARE ROUGH

The object loomed before them, its size and shape warping the very fabric of space around it. Kilometres long, cigar-shaped, and covered in a surface that seemed to absorb all light, it hung in the void like a monolith of darkness. The crew stared at it from Star's bridge, a collective chill running down their spines. There was something deeply wrong about this thing, something that spoke to a primal part of their minds, warning them that they were in the presence of an ancient and malevolent force.

"Star, what are we looking at?" Alex asked, his voice barely concealing the unease that gripped him.

Star's voice was hesitant. "I'm... not certain," she admitted. "There are similarities in its construction to the technology within the mega-structure, but it's different. Cruder, yet more advanced in a way I can't fully comprehend. It's like looking at a twisted reflection of something familiar."

Shanice shivered, wrapping her arms around herself as if to ward off a sudden chill. "It feels... alive," she whispered, her gaze locked on the viewscreen. "Like it's watching us."

Rafen sat hunched over in his seat, his eyes squeezed shut, sweat beading on his brow. He could feel it too, a presence that pressed against his mind like a weight. It was cold, methodical, and utterly devoid of empathy or emotion. It was as if the object itself was a predator, and they were the prey caught in its gaze.

"It's ancient," Rafen managed to say through gritted teeth. "Old and powerful... and it's aware of us."

The bridge fell silent; the crew exchanging uneasy glances. The object was so still, so silent, yet it radiated a sense of imminent threat that made every second feel like an eternity.

Suddenly, Yana's voice crackled over the comms, her tone strained and filled with a cold detachment that they had never heard from her before. "Attention, Star and crew. This is Yana."

"Yana?" Alex responded, a note of hope in his voice. "What is that thing? What are we dealing with?"

Yana's holographic form appeared on the viewscreen, her face solemn and uncharacteristically expressionless. "I have accessed the ancient archives," she said slowly, her voice echoing with a mechanical precision. "This object is a remnant of the ancient enemy, the adversaries of the Celestials. It is a probe, a harbinger of their return. I have closed off the mega-structure for security. None shall enter or leave until the threat is neutralised."

"Yana, you have to help us," Shanice urged, panic creeping into her voice. "We can't handle this alone!"

"I'm sorry," Yana continued, her voice devoid of emotion. "There is no help I can offer. The protocols dictate that such a threat must be isolated and contained. You will not survive. Your sacrifice will be noted in the archives."

The connection cut off, and the screen went dark. The crew was left in stunned silence, the enormity of their situation settling over them like a shroud. Yana, the guardian of the mega-structure, had abandoned them. They were on their own, facing an enemy that even the Celestials had feared.

"Great," J'Coub muttered, his voice tight with fear. "Just great. We're supposed to just die here? Is that it?"

"We're not dead yet," Alex snapped, though his eyes were glued to the viewscreen, to the ominous shape that still hung motionless before them. "Star, can we move? Get us out of here."

Star's systems whirred in response, but she hesitated. "I'm attempting to break away," she said, her voice strained. "But the gravity around the object is fluctuating. It's like it's pulling us in."

The ship shuddered as Star strained against the pull, her engines firing in an effort to push them away from the probe. But it was as if they were caught in a web, the gravity around the object warping and bending, keeping them in place.

"Something's happening," Rafen whispered, his eyes wide and glazed with terror. "I can feel it... it's scanning us."

A low hum filled the air, growing in intensity as the probe seemed to awaken, its surface rippling with an unnatural energy. The darkness that cloaked it began to shift, patterns of light and shadow dancing across its hull in a hypnotic display.

"It's searching," Rafen said through clenched teeth, his hands clutching his head as if to block out the presence invading his mind. "It's searching for something..."

"Star, we need to break free," Alex urged, his voice tight with fear. "Now!"

"I'm trying," Star replied, her voice strained with effort. "But it's holding us in place."

The hum grew louder, resonating through the hull of the ship and into their very bones. The thing's energy flared, and a blinding light erupted from its surface, enveloping Star in a beam that seemed to pierce through her very core.

"Brace yourselves!" Star shouted, her voice filled with a rare note of panic.

The ship shuddered violently as the beam cut through one of her tentacles, severing it in a single, clean stroke. The tentacle floated away, a dark shape drifting into the void as Star's systems sparked and groaned in agony.

"Damage to secondary systems," Star reported, her voice trembling with pain. "I'm... I'm compromised."

"Star!" Shanice cried out, her hands gripping the console in front of her. "Are you okay?"

"I'm... I'm functioning," Star replied, though there was a note of strain in her voice that betrayed the severity of the damage. "But we're not going anywhere. Not until we break free."

The beam retracted, but the object remained ominously still, its surface now pulsating with a dark, malevolent energy. The sense of being watched, of being analysed and dissected, was overwhelming.

"It's... it's a probe," Rafen gasped, his voice breaking with the strain of what he was sensing. "It's... it's just a probe."

"Just a probe?" J'Coub repeated, his voice tinged with disbelief. "If that's just a probe, then what the hell is it probing for?"

"I don't know," Rafen said, his eyes wild with fear. "But it's... it's something ancient. Something that's been waiting for a very long time."

"We need to destroy it," Sorah said, her voice calm and measured despite the tension that filled the room. "Before it can send any information back to whoever sent it."

"Agreed," Alex said, his jaw set. "Star, target all weapons on that thing. We need to take it out before it can do any more damage."

Star hesitated for a moment, her systems buzzing with activity as she aimed her weapons at the probe. "Targeting," she confirmed, her voice devoid of its usual confidence. "But I can't guarantee it will be enough."

"Do it," Alex ordered, his voice hard. "Fire."

Star's weapons blazed to life, beams of energy and missiles streaking toward the probe. But as they neared, the probe's surface shimmered, and a dark energy field erupted around it, absorbing the impact of the attack with an eerie silence.

"Nothing," Shanice said, her voice filled with horror. "It didn't even scratch it."

The probe remained still, its energy field glowing with a dark, unholy light. It was as if it were toying with them, allowing them to see just how powerless they were against it.

Rafen let out a strangled cry, his body convulsing as he clutched his head. "It's... it's in my mind," he gasped, his voice filled with agony. "It's... showing me things..."

"Rafen!" Sorah shouted, moving to his side. "What is it showing you?"

He shook his head violently, his eyes wide and unfocused. "Darkness... destruction... death. I've seen it before. Drowning in the dark. It's... it's like it's showing me what it did... to others... to worlds..."

"Star, we need to break free," Alex urged, his voice filled with a growing sense of desperation. "We can't stay here. We have to get out."

"I'm trying," Star replied, her voice trembling with fear and pain. "But it's holding us. I can't break free."

The probe pulsed with energy, and the surrounding gravity intensified, pulling Star closer. The ship shuddered and groaned as she fought against the pull, her systems straining to keep them from being drawn into the dark maw of the probe.

"Prepare for emergency warp," Alex ordered, his voice tight. "We need to get as far away from this thing as possible."

"Calculating," Star said, her voice laced with urgency. "But I can't guarantee it will work. The probe's gravity field is distorting the surrounding space."

"Do it anyway," Alex commanded. "We don't have a choice."

As Star began to initiate the warp sequence, the probe's energy surged, the darkness around it deepening as it prepared to unleash another attack. Rafen screamed, his body convulsing with the force of the psychic assault, his mind flooded with images of death and destruction, of worlds consumed by the ancient enemy that had sent this probe.

"Rafen, hold on!" Shanice shouted, reaching out to him. "We're getting out of here!"

But Rafen could barely hear her. His mind was drowning in the darkness, the malevolent presence of the probe pressing down on him like a weight. He could feel its hatred, its hunger, its desire to destroy and consume.

And then, with a suddenness that took his breath away, it all stopped.

The probe went silent, its energy field retracting as it drifted back into the void. The sense of being watched, of being analysed, was gone, leaving behind an emptiness that was almost worse.

"What's happening?" Alex demanded, his eyes locked on the viewscreen. "Why did it stop?"

"I... I don't know," Star replied, her voice filled with confusion. "It's... it's gone dormant."

"It's like it just... lost interest," J'Coub said, his voice filled with disbelief.

"No," Rafen whispered, his voice trembling. "It's not that. It's... it's because it got what it wanted."

The crew turned to look at him, their expressions a mix of confusion and fear.

"What do you mean?" Sorah asked, her voice calm but laced with urgency.

Rafen swallowed hard, his eyes haunted. "It was scanning us... studying us. And now... it knows everything. It knows about Star, about the city, about... everything."

A heavy silence fell over the bridge as the full weight of his words sank in. The probe hadn't attacked them, hadn't destroyed them, because it didn't need to. It had already accomplished its mission. It had gathered all the information it needed and was now ready to send it back to whoever, or whatever, had sent it.

"We need to destroy it," Alex said, his voice filled with grim determination. "Now. Before it can transmit what it found."

"Agreed," Star said, her systems already charging for another attack. "Targeting all weapons, I am sending everything I have towards the same location. If this doesn't work, it was a pleasure knowing you all."

As they prepared to make their move, the probe remained ominously still, its dark surface reflecting the light of the distant stars. It was a silent, malevolent presence, a harbinger of something far worse than they could have ever imagined.

And as they fired on it, the sense of hopelessness hung over them like a shroud, a reminder that this was only the beginning. The ancient enemy was out there, and now it knew they existed.

19. THINGS GET WORSE

The crew huddled around the viewscreen, their eyes glued to the image of the probe as it escaped unscathed once again.

Behind them, the mega-structure's surface shifted and transformed. What had once been a symbol of hope and refuge was now a fortress, an impenetrable stronghold that had sealed itself off from the universe. The smooth, sleek surface of the Dyson sphere sprouted deadly looking weapons points, bristling with energy. The structure's doors were closing, massive panels sliding into place as a shimmering blue shield flickered into existence around it.

"Oshman, do you read me?" Alex called into the comms, his voice edged with urgency. "What's happening in there?"

There was a burst of static, followed by Oshman's voice, strained and filled with frustration. "We're being pulled inside towards the city," he reported. "Some kind of tractor beam has locked onto our ships. We're trying to break free, but it's too strong."

"Damn it," Alex muttered under his breath, watching as the last of the doors sealed shut, cutting off any hope of reaching their friends. "Yana has locked them in. They're trapped."

"That shield looks like it could withstand a full-scale assault," Shanice observed, her voice laced with disbelief. "We couldn't get through even if we wanted to."

"And it gets worse," J'Coub added grimly, his eyes scanning the readings on his console. "That probe is recharging. It's preparing for another attack."

They turned their attention back to the probe, still looming in the void like a harbinger of doom. It remained eerily silent, but the energy readings emanating from it were spiking. It was gearing up for something, and they had no idea what.

"Star, can we get a lock on its systems?" Sorah asked, her voice calm but tense.

"I'm trying," Star replied, her voice strained with the effort. "But it's like nothing I've ever encountered. Its technology is... alien in every sense of the word. There's no familiar pattern to follow."

"Then we hit it again with everything we've got," Alex said, his voice hard. "We need to take this thing out before it can fire again. Target a different area, fire and repeat, change targets every volley."

"Understood," Star responded. "Preparing rail guns and anti-matter torpedoes."

The ship shuddered as her weapons powered up, the hum of energy filling the bridge. Star manoeuvred into position, the crew bracing themselves for the onslaught that was about to come.

"Ready to fire on your mark," Sorah reported, her hands steady on the weapons controls.

"Mark," Alex ordered.

The rail guns fired first, unleashing a barrage of high-velocity projectiles that streaked toward the probe. They struck its hull with a resounding impact, the force of the blows shaking the object, but it remained unscathed. The anti-matter torpedoes followed, their payloads detonating against the probe's surface in a brilliant burst of light.

For a moment, it seemed as though they had made progress. The probe shuddered, its energy field flickering as it absorbed the impact. But then, just as quickly, the field stabilised, and the probe continued its silent vigil, seemingly unbothered by the attack.

"Direct hit," Star reported, her voice tinged with disbelief. "But... no damage. It absorbed the energy."

"Damn it," Alex swore, slamming his fist against the console. "We need to find a way to breach its defences. What about the grapplers? Can we pull it apart?"

"I can try," Star said, though there was a note of doubt in her voice. "But I don't know if it will work."

"Do it," Alex ordered. "We're out of options."

Star manoeuvred closer to the probe, her tentacles extending toward it with the intention of latching onto its surface and tearing it apart. But as soon as she made contact, the probe's energy field pulsed, sending a shockwave through Star's systems.

The ship convulsed, alarms blaring as her hull groaned under the strain. One of her grapplers shattered, the metal snapping with a sickening crack as it was repelled by the probe's defences.

"Damage to targeting sensors," Star reported, her voice trembling. "I... I can't maintain a lock."

"Pull back," Alex shouted, his voice filled with urgency. "Get us out of here!"

Star tried to retreat, her engines firing in a desperate attempt to put distance between them and the probe. But the object pulsed again, its gravitational pull intensifying, drawing them closer even as they fought to break free.

"We're not getting away," Shanice said, her voice edged with panic. "It's pulling us in!"

"Reroute power to the engines," Sorah ordered, her fingers flying over the controls. "We need to get some distance!"

"I'm trying," Star said, her voice strained with pain. "But it's like fighting a black hole."

The ship shuddered again, and another of her tentacles was severed, drifting away into the void like a piece of shrapnel. Star let out a pained cry, her systems flickering as she struggled to maintain control.

"We can't keep this up," J'Coub said, his voice filled with grim resignation. "We're outmatched."

Alex gritted his teeth, his mind racing as he searched for a solution. They couldn't fight this thing head-on; it was too powerful. They needed to find a way to exploit its weaknesses, to hit it where it hurt.

And then it came to him. An idea, reckless and dangerous, but it might just be their only chance.

"Maybe it won't recognise something small as a threat," he said slowly, his eyes narrowing as he considered the plan forming in his mind. "We could suit up, spacewalk over to it, and plant explosives directly on its hull."

"Are you insane?" Shanice demanded, turning to face him. "That thing is practically a living fortress. You wouldn't stand a chance."

"We don't have a choice," Alex said, his voice hard. "We can't get through its defences with the weapons we have. But maybe, just maybe, we can slip past its sensors undetected if we're small enough. Explosives, corrosives, even samples of the virus that ate away the mining station. We dump as much as we can on anything that looks vaguely important!"

"I'm going with you," Rafen said suddenly, his voice quiet but filled with determination.

Alex turned to him, surprise flickering across his face. "Rafen, no. It's too dangerous."

"I can help," Rafen insisted, his eyes dark and resolute. "I've been feeling... something. I think I can use my abilities to hide us, to make it so the probe doesn't sense us. It's worth a try."

Alex hesitated, his instincts screaming at him to say no, to protect Rafen from the danger they were facing. But he could see the resolve in the young man's eyes, the determination to do something, anything, to help. And maybe, just maybe, he was right.

"Alright," Alex said finally. "But you stick close to me. Buddy, you're coming too."

Buddy's form shimmered and shifted, morphing into the shape of a space suit that enveloped Rafen's body. Buddy beeped, his voice tinged with a mechanical seriousness.

"Shanice," Alex said, turning to her. "You take the helm. Provide a distraction and then get the hell out if things go south."

Shanice opened her mouth to protest but then nodded, her eyes hard. "Got it. Just don't do anything stupid."

"No promises," Alex said with a grim smile. "Sorah, J'Coub, you're on manual control of the weapons. Keep it busy while we get into position."

They moved quickly, donning their space suits and preparing

for the treacherous journey ahead. The airlock hissed open, revealing the void of space beyond, the probe's dark form looming ominously in the distance.

"Ready?" Alex asked, his voice steady despite the pounding of his heart.

"Ready," Rafen said, his voice filled with a calm determination that surprised even himself.

"Alright," Alex said, taking a deep breath. "Let's do this."

They stepped out into the void, their bodies floating weightlessly as they pushed off from Star's hull. The ship shuddered behind them, Star's systems groaning as she continued to struggle against the probe's pull.

The journey across the empty expanse was harrowing, every moment filled with the tension of knowing they were exposed, vulnerable. The probe loomed ahead, its surface a twisted, alien landscape that defied understanding.

Rafen closed his eyes, reaching out with his mind, feeling for the presence that lurked within the probe. It was there, cold and calculating, but he focused on blocking their presence, hiding them within the folds of its own awareness. It was like slipping through a net, avoiding the strands that sought to ensnare them.

"Keep moving," Alex urged, his voice a whisper in Rafen's ear. "Almost there."

They dodged debris, the remnants of Star's tentacles and fragments of shattered drones that drifted in the void. The probe's energy flared occasionally, a reminder of the power that lay dormant beneath its surface, ready to strike at any moment.

As they neared the probe, Alex spotted a series of indentations along its hull, potential weak points where they could plant the explosives. He gestured to Rafen, signalling for him to follow.

"Plant the charges here," Alex instructed, his voice calm but edged with tension. "We need to set them deep enough to breach the outer hull."

Rafen nodded, his hands steady as he worked. Buddy's form adjusted around him, assisting with the placement of the charges, moulding itself into the shape of tools as needed. They worked quickly, knowing that every second counted.

The surface of the probe was cold, unnaturally so, and Rafen could feel the malevolent presence pressing against his mind, testing his defences. He gritted his teeth, focusing on the task at hand, on keeping them hidden.

"Almost there," Alex said, his eyes scanning the probe for any signs of activity. "Just a little longer."

Rafen nodded, his breathing shallow as he placed the last of the charges. He could feel the weight of the void pressing down on him, the sense of being watched, hunted. The probe was alive in a way he couldn't fully comprehend, a dark intelligence that lurked just beyond the edge of his perception.

"We're set," he said finally, his voice barely a whisper. "Now what?"

"Now we get out of here," Alex replied, his voice tense. "And hope this works."

They turned to make their way back to Star, moving as quickly and quietly as they could. The surrounding void was eerily silent, the probe's energy pulsing softly like the heartbeat of some ancient beast.

As they reached the halfway point, the probe suddenly shuddered, its surface rippling as if sensing their presence. A low hum filled the air, growing in intensity, and Rafen felt a surge of panic rise within him.

"It knows we're here," he said, his voice tight with fear. "It's waking up."

"Move!" Alex shouted, pushing off from the probe's surface with all his strength. "Get back to Star, now!"

They launched themselves into the void, the probe's energy field flaring to life behind them. It pulsed with a dark, ominous light, the sense of malevolence growing as it began to scan for them, searching for the intruders that had dared to breach its defences.

Rafen pushed his mind to its limits, throwing up every barrier he could think of, every defence against the probing tendrils of the entity's awareness. He could feel its frustration, its anger, as it struggled to locate them.

"We're almost there," Alex urged, his voice filled with a mix of hope and desperation. "Just keep moving!"

Star loomed ahead, her hull scarred and battered. The airlock was open, waiting for them, and they pushed themselves toward it with every ounce of strength they had left.

The airlock loomed closer, and for a fleeting moment, it seemed they might just make it. Rafen could feel the strain in his muscles, the burn of fatigue as he pushed himself through the vacuum of space. The void around them was a swirling chaos of debris and shimmering energy, the probe's awareness pressing down on them like a physical weight.

Just as Rafen reached the airlock, a shockwave rippled through space. The probe's energy field flared violently, its pulse sending a surge of force that knocked them off course. Rafen was flung toward the airlock, colliding with the frame, but he managed to catch hold and pull himself inside.

"Alex!" he shouted, turning back just in time to see the captain spinning out of control, the wave of energy sending him tumbling away from the airlock.

Rafen reached out, his fingers grasping at the emptiness, but

Alex was too far, his form shrinking against the backdrop of the probe's dark silhouette.

"Rafen, get inside!" Alex's voice crackled through the comms, his tone filled with command and urgency. "Shut the airlock, now!"

Rafen hesitated, torn between the order and his instinct to help. But the urgency in Alex's voice left no room for argument.

"Do it!" Alex barked. "That's an order!"

With a wrenching sense of guilt, Rafen hit the airlock controls, the hatch sealing shut with a hiss. He slumped against the wall, his heart pounding in his chest as he struggled to breathe, the reality of what had just happened sinking in.

"Star," Alex's voice came through the comms, steady despite the chaos. "I'm not going to make it inside. But we need to finish this."

"Alex, no," Star's voice trembled, the pain in her tone palpable. "You have to find a way back. We can't do this without you."

"You can," Alex replied firmly. "You have to. I'm going to make my way to a safer section of the hull and find cover. Once I'm there, fire the charges."

"No," Rafen whispered, his voice cracking as he gripped the console in front of him. "We can't leave you out there."

"You don't have a choice," Alex shot back, his tone leaving no room for argument. "This is our only chance to destroy that thing. You know it as well as I do."

Rafen felt a surge of desperation, his mind racing for another solution, any solution that wouldn't leave Alex stranded on the hull. But he knew, deep down, that this was their only shot.

"Shanice," Alex continued, his voice softening as he addressed her. "You have the helm. Keep Star safe and get the crew out of here if things go south."

"Alex," Shanice's voice came through, a tremor in her normally steady tone. "You better make it back. You hear me?"

"I hear you," Alex said, a faint smile in his voice. "I'll find a way."

The comms went silent for a moment, the weight of what was happening pressing down on them all. Outside, the probe continued to pulse with energy, its malevolent presence a constant reminder of the danger they were in.

"All right," Alex said finally, his voice hardening with resolve. "Get ready to fire on my mark. I'll give you the signal once I'm in position."

Rafen watched the viewscreen, his heart in his throat as he saw Alex pushing himself along the hull of Star, making his way to a more shielded section near the ship's stern. The sense of helplessness was almost suffocating, the knowledge that they could do nothing but wait.

"Alex," Star's voice came through, her tone softer now, almost pleading. "Please... be careful."

"I will," Alex replied, his voice filled with a calm determination. "I promise."

The seconds stretched into what felt like hours, the tension in the air so thick it was almost tangible. Rafen could feel the probe's awareness probing at the edges of his mind, its frustration and anger growing as it searched for them.

"Almost there," Alex's voice crackled through the comms. "Just... a little... further..."

He reached the section of the hull he had been aiming for, pressing himself flat against the metal, trying to make himself as small and unnoticeable as possible.

"All right," he said, his breathing heavy. "I'm in position. Fire the charges."

Shanice hesitated, her hand hovering over the controls. "Alex..."

"Do it," Alex ordered, his voice filled with a quiet finality. "Now."

With a shaky breath, Shanice activated the detonator. The charges went off in a brilliant flash of light; the explosion tearing through the probe's hull. The energy field around it flickered and cracked, the force of the blast sending shockwaves rippling through the void.

For a moment, it seemed to work. The probe shuddered, its surface warping and distorting as the charges ripped through it. The energy that had been building up within it pulsed and then collapsed in on itself, the probe imploding with a soundless roar that echoed through the emptiness of space.

The crew watched in stunned silence as the probe was reduced to a cloud of debris, the darkness that had surrounded it dissipating into the void.

"We did it," Shanice whispered, her voice filled with disbelief. "We actually did it."

"Alex," Star's voice came through, tinged with a mix of hope and fear. "We're clear. The probe is destroyed. You can move."

There was a long pause, the comms filled with static and the distant hum of Star's systems. Then, finally, Alex's voice crackled through, weak but alive.

"Roger that," he said, his voice strained. "I'm... I'm on my way back. Just... give me a minute."

Rafen let out a breath he hadn't realized he'd been holding, relief flooding through him as he watched the viewscreen. Alex was moving, slowly but surely, making his way back along the hull.

"Take your time," Star said gently, her voice filled with a warmth that belied the tension of the situation. "We're here. We're not going anywhere."

"Good to know," Alex replied, a hint of a smile in his voice. "Because I'm not planning on doing that again anytime soon."

As they watched, Alex continued his treacherous journey across the hull, his movements slow and deliberate as he navigated the twisted metal and debris. Every second felt like an eternity, but he was moving, and that was enough.

"Almost there," Star murmured, her voice filled with an unspoken plea. "Just a little further, Alex. You're almost home."

Rafen's heart pounded in his chest as he watched Alex draw closer to the airlock, his breathing shallow as he willed the captain to make it.

Alex reached the outside of the airlock, his breaths coming in ragged gasps. Every muscle in his body screamed in protest, but he pushed forward, driven by sheer will. His fingers latched onto the edge of the airlock frame, the cold metal a lifeline in the void of space.

"Almost there," he muttered to himself, each word a small victory against the fear that still gnawed at the back of his mind. He could see the faint glow of the airlock's interior light, the promise of safety and his crew's worried faces just a few feet away.

Inside Star, the crew watched with bated breath as he reached out, his hand hovering inches away from the hatch controls.

But just as his fingers brushed the panel, a sudden, violent pulse of dark energy erupted from the remains of the probe. It was like a wave of shadow, a rippling current that surged through the void, reaching out with a cold, hungry intent. Alex felt it before he saw it, a prickling sensation that raced up his spine, freezing him in place.

"Alex, look out!" Rafen's voice crackled over the comms, filled with panic and urgency.

Alex turned just in time to see the wave of energy hurtling toward him. It was a mass of swirling darkness, tendrils of shadow that writhed and twisted as they closed the distance between them. There was no time to react, no chance to move. The energy hit him like a tidal wave, wrapping around his body and yanking him away from the airlock with a force that left him breathless.

"Alex!" Star's voice cried out, filled with horror and desperation.

The crew watched in stunned silence as the dark energy pulled Alex away from the airlock, dragging him back toward the ruins of the probe. His body was enveloped in the shadowy tendrils, his limbs pinned as he was drawn further and further away from the ship.

"Captain!" Shanice shouted, her hands flying over the controls as she tried to adjust Star's trajectory to follow him. "Hold on!"

But it was like fighting against a riptide. The probe, or what remained of it, was exerting a force that Star's damaged systems couldn't counteract. The ship lurched as she tried to move closer, her engines straining against the pull.

Rafen pressed his hands against the viewscreen, his eyes wide with terror. "It's not dead," he whispered, his voice trembling. "Something is still alive."

The core of the probe had become visible now, a dark, pulsating mass at the centre of the debris field. It was consuming everything around it, pulling in fragments of shattered metal and technology, absorbing them into its swirling vortex of energy. It was rebuilding itself, atom by atom, drawing in the remnants of its shattered form to create something new.

And it was pulling Alex straight toward it.

"Star, do something!" Sorah barked, her voice edged with a rare note of fear. "Get him out of there!"

"I'm trying," Star replied, her voice filled with anguish. "But I can't break through its energy field. It's too strong."

"Alex!" Shanice shouted again, her voice breaking as she watched him being dragged further away. "You have to fight it!"

Alex struggled against the pull, his arms and legs straining against the tendrils of dark energy that held him fast. He could feel the core's malevolent presence, a cold intelligence that pressed against his mind like a vice. It was aware of him, analysing him, deciding what to do with this new threat.

He gritted his teeth, every muscle in his body screaming as he fought to break free. But the energy around him tightened, squeezing the air from his lungs as it dragged him inexorably toward the probe's core. He felt immense cold biting into him as his suit began to dissolve slowly, its regenerative abilities sealing the breaches only to be eaten away again.

"Hold on, Alex," Star pleaded, her voice a mix of desperation and determination. "We're not leaving you."

But even as she spoke, the core pulsed with a surge of power, the dark energy around it growing stronger, more focused. It was pulling him in with a terrifying inevitability, drawing him closer and closer to the swirling mass of shadow and debris.

The crew could only watch in horror, their helplessness a heavy weight on their chests as they saw their captain being pulled toward what was left of the probe. Every attempt to move closer, to fight against the dark force, was met with a resistance that Star couldn't overcome in her weakened state.

"Captain," Rafen whispered, his voice breaking. "Please..."

Alex turned his head, straining against the energy that bound him, his eyes locking onto the viewscreen. He could see the crew, their faces filled with fear and anguish, could hear Star's voice trembling as she called out to him. And he knew, in that moment, that there was nothing they could do.

"Stay with Star," he managed to say, his voice barely a whisper through the comms. "Protect the crew. You have to get out of here..."

"No!" Shanice cried, slamming her fist against the console. "We're not leaving you behind!"

"You don't have a choice," Alex replied, his voice steady despite the pain that laced every word. "Get them away from here. That's an order."

The surrounding energy tightened, pulling him closer to the core. He could feel its hunger, its desire to consume, to rebuild itself into something far more terrible than before. And he knew, deep down, that this was it.

"Alex," Star's voice came through, choked with emotion. "Please..."

"I know," he said softly, his eyes closing for a brief moment. "I know."

The darkness enveloped him, the swirling tendrils pulling him into the heart of the core. The last thing he saw before the void swallowed him was the crew, their faces etched with horror and grief, and Star's gentle light shining through the darkness.

And then, there was nothing but the cold, endless night.

20. DESPERATION

The moment Alex was swallowed by the darkness, an eerie stillness settled over the bridge of Star. The crew stood in shock, watching in horror as their captain was enveloped by the mass of nanites and dark energy. It was as if time had slowed to a crawl, every second stretching into an eternity as they struggled to comprehend what had just happened.

Star's lights flickered, a soft tremor running through her systems as if she, too, was reeling from the loss. For a moment, there was only silence, a heavy, oppressive weight that pressed down on them all.

Then, with a sudden, violent motion, Buddy moved. His sleek, adaptable form shuddered as he shifted from his vaguely humanoid shape into something more streamlined, more focused. His processors whirred, and without hesitation, he launched himself toward the nearest hull access point.

"Buddy, wait!" Shanice shouted, but it was too late.

Buddy tore through Star's hull with a force that sent a shudder through the entire ship. Metal screamed and twisted, the breach sealing itself almost as soon as it was made. Star reacted instinctively, her self-repair protocols kicking in to seal the tear, but Buddy was already through, a blur of motion as he propelled himself into the void of space.

"Buddy!" Star's voice echoed through the comms, filled with a mix of desperation and anguish. "What are you doing?"

There was no response, only the sight of Buddy streaking toward the dark mass that held Alex within its grasp. His form shimmered and shifted, his sleek exoskeleton reforming to create an aerodynamic shape that cut through the vacuum with ease. He moved with a singular purpose, a determination that was almost palpable, as if he were driven by a force beyond his own programming.

"He's going after Alex," Sorah said, her voice hollow with disbelief. "He's... he's going to try and save him."

"But how?" Rafen whispered, his eyes fixed on the screen. "That thing... it's too powerful."

Sorah shook her head, unable to find the words to respond. They watched in silence as Buddy closed the distance between himself and the mass of nanites and dark energy, a glimmer of hope flickering within them despite the overwhelming despair.

Buddy reached the edge of the dark cloud, his form rippling with energy as he extended tendrils of Flexium nanites from his body. They spread out like a web, reaching into the darkness to combat the malevolent force that held Alex within its grasp. The nanites shimmered with a silver light, a stark contrast to the swirling blackness that surrounded them.

He plunged into the mass, the tendrils of dark energy wrapping around him like a living thing, trying to consume him as it had done with Alex. But Buddy didn't falter. He released a surge of energy, his internal systems pushing to their limits as he poured everything he had into the battle.

The dark energy writhed and twisted, a mass of nanites and

malevolent intent that resisted with a fury born of ancient malice. Buddy felt it pressing against him, probing at his core, seeking to find a way in, to break him down. But he held firm, his Flexium nanites spreading throughout the cloud, counteracting the dark nanites one by one.

It was a battle of wills, a contest between two forces fighting for dominance within the void. Buddy pushed deeper into the cloud, his sensors scanning for any sign of Alex, for any indication that there was still something to save.

The mass of darkness around him pulsed and shifted, the dark energy surging against his efforts. It was like a living thing, a creature of shadow and hunger that sought to consume everything in its path. Buddy could feel its rage, its desire to destroy, but he did not back down. He had a mission, and he would see it through to the end.

The Flexium nanites began to glow brighter, a silver sheen spreading through the darkness as they slowly, methodically counteracted the enemy's influence. It was slow, painstaking work, but Buddy was relentless, his systems pushing to their absolute limits to contain and dismantle the malevolent force.

Slowly, almost imperceptibly, the dark energy began to recede. The mass of nanites and shadow lost some of its cohesion, its tendrils retracting as Buddy's presence overwhelmed it. He could feel it weakening, its power draining as he fought to neutralise it.

It was only then, as the darkness began to thin, that Buddy detected something within the heart of the cloud. A faint, barely perceptible signal that called out to him, a whisper amidst the void.

He pushed forward, his sensors honing in on the source of the signal. The darkness resisted, lashing out with tendrils of energy that clawed at his form, but he pressed on, driven by the need to reach the centre.

As he neared the core of the mass, the dark energy around him faltered, its strength waning. The tendrils withdrew, the cloud of nanites dissipating into nothingness as Buddy's Flexium nanites consumed and neutralised them.

And then, finally, he saw him.

Alex floated in the heart of the dark mass, what remained of his body limp and motionless. The energy that had surrounded him was gone, but the toll it had taken was evident. His suit was in tatters, his form pale and gaunt, as if the life had been drained from him. Half of his body had been eaten away by the dark energy. His eyes were closed, his face eerily peaceful in the stillness of the void.

Buddy reached out, his tendrils wrapping around Alex's form gently, cradling him in a protective cocoon. He could feel the coldness that radiated from him, the absence of life that sent a pang of sorrow through his systems.

Buddy let out a soft mechanical whine.

But there was no response, no sign of life. Buddy ran a scan, searching for any trace of a heartbeat, a pulse, a flicker of consciousness. He found nothing.

The realisation settled over him, a cold, crushing weight that bore down on his circuits. Alex was gone. The darkness had consumed him, taken him away before Buddy could reach him.

For a moment, Buddy simply floated there, holding Alex's body in his grasp, the emptiness of the void pressing in around them. He could feel the data flooding through his systems, the cold, hard facts that told him there was no hope, that there was nothing left to save.

But facts were not emotions, and something deep within Buddy's programming, something that transcended his mechanical nature, refused to accept it. He had failed, and the weight of that failure was almost too much to bear.

Slowly, gently, Buddy began the journey back to Star. He moved with a solemn grace, his form steady and controlled despite the turmoil that raged within him. The crew watched from the viewscreen, their faces etched with grief and disbelief as they saw him approach.

He passed through the tear in Star's hull; the breach sealing itself once more as he reentered the ship. The airlock hissed open, and Buddy floated inside, cradling Alex's body in his grasp.

The crew gathered around as he entered, their expressions a mix of horror and sorrow as they saw the lifeless form of their captain. Rafen stepped forward, his eyes wide and filled with tears as he reached out, his fingers trembling.

"Alex..." he whispered, his voice breaking.

Buddy gently laid Alex's body down on the floor of the airlock, his form shimmering as he shifted back into his usual shape. He knelt beside him, his head bowed, the soft hum of his systems the only sound in the silence.

"He's sorry," Rafen said, his voice a hollow whisper. "He tried... but it was too late."

Star's lights flickered, a soft tremor running through her systems as she processed the scene before her. Her voice came through, a quiet, mournful echo that filled the space.

"He was brave," said softly, her tone filled with a deep, aching sadness. "He fought until the end."

Shanice dropped to her knees, letting out a breath that sounded strangled, her eyes almost blank with shock.

The crew stood in silence, the weight of the loss settling over them like a shroud. They had won the battle, but the cost had been too high, the victory hollow in the face of what they had lost.

Sorah knelt beside Alex, her eyes closed as she placed a hand on his chest, a silent gesture of respect and farewell. "Rest well, Captain," she murmured, her voice trembling. "You did what you had to do."

Rafen turned away, his shoulders shaking as he fought back the tears that threatened to overwhelm him. He had sensed it, the darkness, the malevolence that had taken Alex from them, and he felt powerless in the face of it.

"We should... we should take him to the med bay," J'Coub said quietly, his voice choked with emotion as he rested a hand on Shanice's unmoving shoulder. "We owe him that much."

Buddy nodded, his movements slow and deliberate as he lifted Alex's body once more. He carried him with a gentle care, as if he were holding something precious and fragile, the weight of his grief a silent burden that he bore without complaint.

The crew followed in silence as Buddy made his way through the corridors of Star, the lights dimming in a soft, mournful glow as they passed. The ship itself seemed to be grieving, her systems humming with a quiet sorrow that echoed through the halls.

As they reached the med bay, Buddy laid Alex's remains down on the examination table, his manipulator arms lingering for a moment as if reluctant to let go. He stepped back, his form shimmering as he stood there, his body tilted forward as if his head was bowed.

Star's voice came through, a soft, comforting whisper that filled the space. "He was a good man," she said, her tone filled with a deep, abiding respect. "He gave everything to protect us."

"Yes," Sorah replied, her voice a hollow echo. "He did."

The crew stood around the table in a silent vigil for their fallen captain. The weight of the loss hung heavy in the air, a reminder of the cost of their journey, the sacrifices that had been made.

And in the silence of the med bay, they mourned.

AFTERWORD

Thanks for reading book 2 in Echoes of the Celestials.

Book 3 will be coming in 2025, so please keep your eyes peeled and follow me on Amazon.

As usual ratings and reviews really help an author out, especially new ones like me, so please rate and review on Amazon or Goodreads. Buddy will love you for it!

BOOKS IN THIS SERIES

Echoes of the Celestials

Star's Odyssey

Star's Promise

Star's Universe

Coming 2025

www.ingramcontent.com/pod-product-compliance
Lightning Source LLC
LaVergne TN
LVHW010102170826
845678LV00012B/2216

* 9 7 8 1 7 3 8 5 6 5 3 2 0 *